ON REBEL TURF...

Captain Gringo started to fade back toward the river as the guerrilla stepped into view. But Olivia was sort of new to night fighting. So she whipped the carbine stick up to her shoulder and, for a lady more used to reciting Scripture than using rifles, blew a lung out of the back of the man's rib cage pretty good!

Captain Gringo grunted, "Oh shit!" and stepped out into the moonlight, his gun trained on the two surviving guerrillas posted at the mounted machine gun. He dropped the closer one first as Olivia fired again and sent the other ass-over-tea-kettle into the night.

In the distance he heard a guerrilla shouting, "God damn it, take cover. Don't just stand there like a bunch of bananas waiting to be plucked!"

That was good enough for Captain Gringo. He fired a long withering burst of automatic fire right into the screaming target!

He introduced himself as D. T. David, the Reverend D. T.

Novels by
RAMSAY THORNE

Published by
WARNER BOOKS

Renegade #30

MAYHEM AT MISSION BAY

Ramsay Thorne

WARNER BOOKS

A Warner Communications Company

Warner Books, Inc.
666 Fifth Avenue
New York, N.Y. 10103

 A Warner Communications Company

Printed in the United States of America

First Printing: May, 1985

10 9 8 7 6 5 4 3 2 1

When Captain Gringo said persistent pansies gave him a pain in the ass, he was speaking metaphorically. He'd been in some odd positions indeed since he'd been on the run with a price on his ass. But so far he'd never been either the bugger or buggee in a man-to-man situation, and he wasn't at all interested in learning what either felt like. So when Señorito Romero minced into the main salon of the SS *Trinidad* just after sunset, Captain Gringo slipped out the far door to the promenade deck.

This wasn't saying much. *Trinidad* was only a passenger vessel amidships, between her two big side paddles. Fore and aft of the center island, she was a tramp steamer who poked in and out of many a port of call up and down the Mosquito Coast to take on or drop off more serious cargo. The passenger accommodations above her engine room and bunkers probably helped her owners with the fuel bills and payroll. They didn't seem to care whether their passengers were in a hurry, and should anyone want to get off at a port offering nothing in the way of cargo business, tough shit. But when a knockaround guy needed transportation in a hurry, he took what he could get; and the purser had said they'd be putting in at Limon or, if not Limon, *some* damned Costa Rican port of call, so what the hell.

The tall blond soldier of fortune moved along the port deck as far as it went. Then, cornered between the paddle-wheel box and the rail overlooking the forward well deck, he cupped his hands around a match and lit a claro. Above the chunking of the paddles he heard a girlish voice observe, "Oh, so here you are, Ricardo! Have you been avoiding me, or . . . did you want to meet me out here discreetly?"

Romero's English was almost perfect. From there it was all downhill. Captain Gringo turned his back to the rail to face his gay caballero. Not because he wanted to look at the little creep, but because it made him goosey to have his rump exposed to Romero. The mariposa had first made his

1

desires obvious by grabbing for the much-bigger Yank's
dong under the captain's table at dinner earlier in the
voyage and hadn't kept his hands to himself enough to
matter since.

Señorito Hector Romero was a plump, perfumed little
guy who would have made a short woman had he been
built more in accord with his obvious sexual preferences.
He wore a white linen suit, and his hatless head was
pomaded with Macassar oil so that his slicked-down hair
shone like patent leather. It was too dark out on deck to
tell if he was wearing makeup, but he probably was.
Captain Gringo said, "I came out here to be alone, if it's
all the same to you, Pal."

Romero giggled like a schoolgirl and said, "Oh, I *do*
want to be your pal, Ricardo! Why do you insist on
fighting it? Can't you see it's bigger than both of us?"

Captain Gringo laughed despite himself and said, "Flat-
tery will get you nowhere. Look, Romero, I don't know
how else to put it, but I'm just not your kind of guy."

"Why don't we let *me* be the judge of that?" lisped the
mariposa, adding in a huskier tone: "My stateroom is just
down the deck, and I assure you none of the others will know.
You're afraid your little French sweetheart will be jealous?
Pooh, how is he to find out? Who is going to tell him?"

Captain Gringo laughed again and said, "You, for one, if
you had anything to brag about. But before you and my
sidekick, Gaston, get into a hair-pulling contest over my
fair white body, it's only fair to warn you he likes *girls,*
which is just as lucky for you. Old Gaston fights dirty."

Romero sighed impatiently and insisted, "Pooh, I don't
see why you two are so insistent on this butch act you've
been putting on. Don't you think I've noticed the jealous
looks he's been casting our way every time I try to get next
to you, Ricardo?"

"You know what you are, Romero? You're nuts! Old
Gaston has a wry sense of humor, and it's pretty obvious
what you are. So, if it's any comfort to you, he's been
kidding me about you. He seems to think it would settle
your nerves if somebody shoved an umbrella up your ass
and opened it. But I don't have an umbrella or anything

else I want to shove up your ass, so why don't you go bother someone else? There has to be at least one hard-up guy who's not so particular on a vessel this size, right?"

The pansy pouted and said, "Pooh, I don't want a sordid affair with some mestizo crewman. I want *you*, Ricardo! Can't you see I am crazy about you?"

"Crazy is the word I've been groping for. Can't you see I'm just not interested in your brand of slap and tickle, damn it?"

"I can see you're shy. But if you're not at least bisexual, why did you react so *calmly* to my first discreet advances, Ricardo?"

The big Yank snorted smoke out his nostrils in disgust and replied, "Tactical error, I guess. Beating up a fellow passenger forty miles out to sea could be indiscreet indeed, and what the hell, I've never needed to punch out pansies to prove my manhood to myself. But while we're on the subject, you really are starting to steam me, Romero. So why don't you take a hike before this dumb situation starts getting uncivilized?"

Romero paid no attention to the not-too-friendly warning and insisted, "We won't be putting in to Limon for at least seventy-two hours, Darling. Just give me two or three nights in your big strong arms, and I promise, when we get off in Costa Rican juristiction I shall let you go your way if you no longer want me. On the other hand, if you and Verrier need a hideout, my hacienda near San Jose...."

"Get back to that part about *juristiction*!" Captain Gringo cut in, narrow-eyed indeed. For Gaston Verrier had not signed his right name to the purser's list, and a knockaround guy got good at spotting veiled threats or even, hell, slips of the tongue.

Romero smiled up at him knowingly and said, "Don't worry, Darling. Your secret is safe with me. Heavens, why should I want to turn a hunk like you over to La Policia? I assure you I'd rather have you in *me* than in any old *jail*, eh?"

Captain Gringo kept his voice desperately calm as he asked the mariposa what on earth he was talking about, adding, "My friend, M'sieu Fontleroy, and I are not in any trouble with the police, Chum. We're both free-lance banana brokers, see?''

"Oh, let's go to my stateroom and let me peel your banana *right,* Ricardo mio, or should I call you 'Captain Gringo,' as some of your other admirers do?''

So there it was, out in the open like a wad of warm spit. The taller American stared soberly down at the Costa Rican catamite and said thoughtfully, "You sure must like to swim a lot, Friend.''

Romero didn't even glance over the side as he replied in his prissy self-confident way, "Pooh, I know you too well to worry about you raising a hand to me, Ricardo Walker, alias Captain Gringo! You are, it may be true, a man who had killed in his time. But never at a time that would be *foolish,* eh?''

"I'll have to study on that, Chum. Tell me more about this guy you seem to think I might be. I don't remember signing any name like Walker when we came aboard.''

Romero snickered and said, "How could you have, when there are Reward posters out on you and your French lover all the way from Los Estados Unidos to Brazil? I was in Belize when you two came in aboard that schooner, *La Nombre Nada.* I recognized you at once, but who was *I* to inform the local British constabulary. Do I look British?''

"You look like a sissy, and you're still full of shit.''

"No, I'm not. I take regular enemas, and I assure you I'm cleaner down there than the pussy of that notorious female gunruner you were aboard that schooner with, you mean thing! I know why you have to get off at Belize. I asked around the waterfront. The schooner had salt in her condenser and a cracked mainmast. So your gunrunning chums had to lay up in Belize for repairs longer than you and your little Frenchy thought safe. You boarded this steamer to get back to Costa Rica where the police aren't interested in you—or won't be unless a Costa Rican landowner makes a formal complaint, eh?''

Captain Gringo sighed and said, "Right, you really must be a good swimmer! What charge did you have in mind, rape?''

Romero giggled and said, "Ooh, that sounds heavenly!

I can't wait to feel the thrill of you raping me with your big Yanqui love tool!''

"Glugh!" Captain Gringo grimaced, shaking his head wearily as he added, "Look, Romero, even to save my ass I just couldn't get it stiff enough to shove in *yours*! I'm not trying to brag. I'm just not the kind of guy who goes in for that kind of stuff.''

"You're a professional soldier, aren't you?"

"Sort of. The wars down here aren't run too professionally. But what's that got to do with my being queer for women?''

"Pooh, everyone knows all the great military leaders in history were homosexual, Ricardo. Take Alexander, take Caesar, take Lord Nelson, take—"

"No thanks," Captain Gringo cut in, adding, "I'll stick with Washington, Lee and U.S. Grant if you don't mind, and come to think of it, Nelson's Lady Hamilton was some shemale dish!''

"Oh well, *some* of you are bisexual, except when out at sea, as you may have noticed you happen to be right now, Darling. Come on, let me show you how Lady Hamilton took care of Nelson. We're both a lot prettier than *they* were!''

Captain Gringo knew it would be a waste of time to point out Nelson had fathered a daughter with Lady Hamilton, whatever else he'd gone in for on the side. Guys like Romero just couldn't believe other guys weren't like them no matter how often they got beat up, and, unfortunately, that didn't happen so often as it might because there were simply times when punching out a pansy was more trouble than it was worth.

This was one of them. He knew, and Romero knew he knew, that if a well-known landowner who'd no doubt cabled his expected time of arrival ahead of him down the coast didn't arrive on time, all sorts of people in Costa Rica were going to ask all sorts of questions. Questions a knockaround guy holing up between jobs in one of the few banana republics that didn't have an extradition treaty with Uncle Sam was in no mood to have to answer.

But if he couldn't smack Romero at the moment, he didn't have to listen to any more of this bullshit. So he blew smoke in the little twit's face and said, or growled, "I'm going to my own stateroom. You're not invited. You want to get out of my way?"

But Romero pressed closer, cornering Captain Gringo between the rail and paddle box as he insisted urgently, "Just one time! If you don't like it, I'll let you go, Darling!"

"Hey, I *know* I wouldn't like it; and if you don't let me go right *now* you're fixing to get splinters in your rump, Chump!"

"Oh, don't tease me about my rump, Ricardo! You know what I want in it! I want your big hard penis sliding in and out of my throbbing rectum!"

Captain Gringo decided the best way to handle the lovesick lunatic would be to simply pick him up and stand him to one side out of the way. But as he grabbed the front of Romero's linen jacket by both lapels, another pale form materialized from the shadows behind the mariposa and Captian Gringo just had time to gasp, "No, Gaston, don't do it!" before Gaston did it.

Romero gave a funny little sigh and stared up more blankly than adoringly now, as Captain Gringo held him erect by the front of his clothes. Behind the still-warm and upright corpse, Gaston Verrier, late of the French Foreign Legion, Mexican Field Artillery and too many other outfits to mention, wiped his blade clean on the tails of Romero's jacket as he observed, "Eh bien, it is not easy to hit that nerve on the first thrust, but I am most expert in such matters, non?"

Captain Gringo groaned, "Goddamn it, Gaston, you know I don't go in for cold-blooded murder!" So the smaller, older and often as deadly Frenchman replied, "Oui, that is why I did it, Dick. Obviously *one* of us had to shut him up, and I was becoming très bored with waiting for you to do it as I listened from the other side of the paddle wheel box."

Gaston put the stiletto back in its sheath under the back of his collar as he added, "Why are you clinging to him so possessively, mon old and rare? Don't you know how to get rid of garbage at sea?"

"You crazy little bastard! He's supposed to be getting off with us at Limon in a couple of days! Worse yet, he's supposed to be eating at the skipper's table all the way there! How the fuck are we supposed to explain when he doesn't show up for breakfast in the cold gray dawn?"

Gaston put something in his pocket, reached for the back of Romero's jacket and the seat of his pants and replied, "First things first, mon ami. Let go, damn it."

Captain Gringo did so. Gaston shifted the upright corpse like a barroom bouncer ejecting a drunk from the premises and ejected it over the side. The splash was lost amid the churning of the paddle wheel that it landed just ahead of. Once the big wheel had sucked it under, Captain Gringo thought Gaston was overexplaining as he observed, "Très bien, once the blades have left him bobbing in the wake, pre-chewed for the sharks who always follow ships in these waters, the très ridicule pest will have vanished from this earth as a soap bubble from a child's bubble pipe, non?"

"Didn't you hear what I just said about his friends and relations in Costa Rica, or worse yet, the officers aboard this tub who'll be missing him even sooner?"

"Oui. I heard what *he* was saying, too. Hell hath no fury like a sodomist scorned, and he might well have turned you in at breakfast in any case, Dick. Did I fail to mention we did not fix the purser as we came aboard in Belize?"

"Okay, if he'd snitched on us to underpaid ship's officers, they might have figured the reward money out of their own, but, Jesus, Gaston, we're aboard with no papers that'll really stand up to a close examination, and once the skipper starts to ask questions—"

"We may be safe through breakfast," Gaston cut in, explaining: "I was discussing the late Señorito Romero's perfume with the bartender inside just now. Everyone aboard knows he is, or was, a species of swish. So let us arrange his stateroom in a more convincing manner, non? Come, I took the liberty of helping myself to his key as well as his wallet just now."

Still a lot more worried than the dapper little Frenchman sounded, Captain Gringo followed Gaston along the short promenade to the dead man's locked door. He sweated some more until Gaston had it open without anyone else, so far, having come out on deck. Inside, Gaston switched on the overhead Edison lamp. The both grimaced in disgust as they spotted what was making the place smell so weird. An enema bag hung above the commode and Romero hadn't bothered to flush—in his eagerness to cruise the ship for carnal conquest. As Captain Gringo reached for the flush chain, Gaston snapped, "Mais non! Let the sweet scent of merde mingled with perfume linger as long as possible, Dick! If you were a nosy crewman, would you stick your adorable nose in such an obvious den of perverse desires? Ah, here is what we are looking for, non?"

As he held up the little cardboard sign, "No incomadar, por favor!" Captain Gringo nodded and said, "Yeah, a Don't Disturb sign on a known pansy-boy's door ought to keep them out for a *while*. But even a fruitcake has to eat once in a while, and we're two or three days out of Limon, damn it!"

Gaston handed him the Don't Disturb sign as he began to rummage through Romero's luggage, saying, "Oui, but we only need until noon tomorrow. I heard one of the mates observe we shall be putting in to a place called Mission Bay before then. Naturally, we shall go ashore to stretch our legs, and should the ship leave without us—"

"Damn it, Gaston, they're going to notice if you rifle the guy's luggage!"

"Merde alors, what of it? By the time they get around to breaking in on him and his très mysterious lover, they will have noticed we seem to be missing too, non?"

"Non. I mean it. Leave the guy's stuff alone. You're not the only sneak who thinks ahead in this outfit. There's always an outside chance they'll buy his falling overboard on his own. But not if it's obvious someone *robbed* him, see?"

"Spoilsport." Gaston sighed, closing a Gladstone grip and shoving it back under the bunk as he agreed, "Eh bien, he probably had all his money in his adorable wallet in any case; and should they suspect he got fresh with a crew member, they may *wish* to feel he simply fell overboard. Let us make our way back to the salon and establish it firmly to one and all that neither of us seem to be in the habit of strolling the deck by moonlight with a mariposa!''

They did. They switched off the light, made sure the coast was clear and left the door locked behind them with the Don't Disturb sign hanging on the knob. Then Gaston tossed the key over the rail as they headed along the deck for the salon again.

It was less crowded inside, now. The steamer was rolling a bit in the ground swells of an otherwise calm tropic night; and anyone who had anyone to sleep with, or even a good book to read, had retired to their own staterooms. There were some men playing cards at a corner table, and a couple of mousy-looking women sat together at another, not looking up as the two soldiers of fortune came in. As they bellied up to the bar together, the Jamaican bartender looked mildly surprised to see them. Before he could ask any questions a guy with hair on his chest might not want to answer, Gaston said, ''We both require très tall gins avec tonic, mon ami. When there is no other action on a ship, there is nothing for men of the world to do at this hour but *drink*, non?''

The black bartender grinned knowingly as he proceeded to fill their orders, saying, ''Ain't that the truth, Mon? This sure has been a mightly quiet voyage this time. Sometimes we do get some fancy gals going up or down the coast, but the only gals aboard who ain't got proper escorts be them two dried-up bitty gals in the corner behind you. We, ah, are talking about fancy *gals*, ain't we?''

Captain Gringo chuckled easily, though he felt sort of tense, as he replied, ''You noticed that swish that was in here awhile ago, eh? Where'd he go? I'm not sure I'm that desperate yet, but they say we won't reach Limon for another three nights or so!''

The bartender laughed in the way most men laughed when discussing men like Romero and said, ''He's all yours, Mon. I've sailed me some high seas and I've been in some dry ports. But I ain't never been *that* desperate yet!''

Then he slid the drinks across the mahogany as he spoiled it all by adding, "I did notice him trying to start up with you, Mister Crawford. Tell the truth, I was a mite concerned when I saw him follow you out on deck before. I mean, that bitty fruit was really asking for it, picking on a rosy-cheeked boy as big as *you*!''

Captain Gringo took a sip of his drink before he asked with a thoughtful frown, "Really? Funny, I didn't notice him on deck just now. I was, ah, looking to see if anything in a *skirt* was maybe out there in a lonesome deck chair.''

The bartender shrugged, then moved down the long bar to take care of a pea-jacketed crewman who'd just come in. Captain Gringo muttered to Gaston, "This ain't gonna work. They've made the connection, damn it!''

But Gaston soothed, "A conscience is not a thing for a man in our line of work to carry about with him, my guilty child. The observant bartender noticed the swish making the eyes of goo-goo at you. But what of it? You are here drinking with me and the rest of the boys right now, hein?''

"Yeah, and if he wonders why Romero never came back in . . .''

"Stop looking so tense, Dick. Why should we know or care where the sodomist is, avec whom, doing what, hein? Maybe we had better make the pass of gallantry at the adorable frumps in the corner, though, if we wish to establish our credentials more firmly as true men of the usual type, non?''

Captain Gringo could see the two frumps they were talking about in the mirror over the bar, so he said, "Non, they're both old bags, and worse yet, they don't look like they want to get picked up.''

"How do you know? It may simply be more difficult for such sad individuals to start a shipboard romance. But every woman who can read has read of shipboard romances, and they are up unusually late for two femmes who do not seem interested in serious drinking, hein?''

"Never mind about them, damn it. Tell me some more about this Mission Bay we may make it to just in time."

Gaston shrugged and said, "I have never been there. Since it has an English name and lies along the Mosquito Coast like Bluefields or Greytown, it may be one of those très tedious little coaling stations the British grabbed back in the forties when you Yankees were too wrapped up in the Mexican War to notice people ignoring your so-called Monroe Doctrine."

He took a judicious sip of gin and tonic before he elaborated, "It's probably a port seized from Nicaragua. Victoria grabbed a très formidable bit of real estate in bits and pieces . . . oh, I think it was in forty-six. Oui, that was when the Royal Navy convinced Nicaragua they needed coaling stations for their busy little battleships more than Nicaragua really did and—"

"Damn it, I heard all about the Nicaraguan Wars that time we were stuck in Greytown, and in case you've forgotten, both the Brits and Nicaraguans, both sides, are mad at us right now!"

"True, but who is expecting us to disembark at Mission Bay, since we've never heard of the place before? While, on the other hand, the fruitcake we just threw to the sharks has friends who may be meeting this jolly boat further down the coast, hein?"

Captain Gringo swore under his breath and said, "Okay, we'd better get off sooner. But after we're in Mission Bay, how the hell are we supposed to get *out*? It's the dry season, so the Leonistos and Granaderos will be at it again in Nicaragua. We've found out the hard way we don't want to join either side in that ongoing mess. But if we stay put in a British Crown Colony so small it's not on the larger-scale maps, we'll be picked up in no time."

"Picky, picky, picky. Was it not you, Dick, who introduced me to the droll Yankee observation a man can only eat an apple one bite at a time? Let us get out of this mess before we worry about the *next* one, hein? If Mission Bay is a seaport, other vessels must put in there. We got aboard this one easily enough. Let us simply get off before the skipper throws us in irons and . . . Heads up, our friend is coming back!'' He waited until the bartender was closer before he added with a smile, ''Where have you been, my long-lost child? Can you not see our glasses have perished for their country?''

The Jamaican grinned back as he started building them new gin and tonics. He waited until he had before he leaned forward and muttered, ''Can you believe it, that bitty Costa Rican fruit fly has hisself a lover in his stateroom!''

Captain Gringo shrugged and said, ''No shit?''

Which made the bartender laugh like hell. He poured himself a drink as he winked and softly said, ''That's the truth. Deckhand I was just talking to down there say you can smell shit and perfume clean out on deck and, get this, the bodacious bugger has the Don't Disturb sign out, like he means to make a *night* of it! Ain't that disgusting?''

Captain Gringo shrugged and said, ''Well, some guys collect stamps and some guys have other hobbies. Where'd that other crew member go just now? Back to ask for sloppy seconds?''

''I hope not! I showers regular with that boy! He just ducked in for a quick drink. Ain't supposed to, but who's to report him? He say he'll keep an eye on the sissy boy's quarters as he walks his deck watch. Skipper will want to know, Do we have anyone *else* like that aboard. Ain't much the owners will let us do about what passengers does in their own staterooms. But you gotta keep an eye on queers aboard ship. They causes more trouble than women, and you know how much trouble *women* cause at sea!''

Gaston turned his back to the bar to stare owlishly at the two spinsterly types in the far corner as he mused aloud, ''Mais non, but it might be très amusé to find out.''

Then, before Captain Gringo could stop him, the little Frenchman was on his way over as the two women, having spotted him coming, seemed to cower back in their seats like crayfish trying to back into holes that just weren't there.

Captain Gringo didn't follow. He didn't want either dame screaming down at him from the ceiling. He looked wearily at the bartender and said, "What can I tell you? He's French."

The Jamaican laughed easily and said, "He sure ain't no *sissy* Frenchman, then, Mon! You'd have to like gals a *lot* to start up with a pair as cold-natured-looking as them two!"

"Yeah, they do seem sort of snooty," said Captain Gringo as Gaston sat down by them, uninvited, and began a line they couldn't make out from the bar, which was probably just as well. Captain Gringo asked the Jamaican what the story was on the two severely dressed and obviously Hispanic broads. The bartender shrugged and said, "They's sisters, I think. Both widows with business in both Belize and Costa Rica. Don't know what kind. They ain't much for chatting with the hired help or, come to think of it, anyone else, Mon. This the first time I've ever seen another passenger start up with either one and, Do Jesus, look at that Frenchy go! He got the older one grinning at him like a shit-eating dog!"

Captain Gringo had to chuckle. For it was true the older and, if possible, more formidable-looking of the two middle-aged, pure-Spanish-looking dames was not only laughing openly at something Gaston had just said, but was poking at him with her folded fan as the other—having produced her own black lace fan from somewhere among her widow's weeds—was looking away from the two of them as she fluttered her fan, and eyelashes, in Captain Gringo's general direction.

Not directly at him, of course; no well-brought-up Hispanic woman or even a less-than-desperate whore ever looked directly at a man she hadn't been introduced to. But as the bartender whispered, "*Go*, Mon! Don't you know the Spanish come-on when you sees it?" He decided he'd better at least smile at her, lest the crew start wondering about his masculinity again.

She wasn't looking at him, it seemed, when he smiled. But she sure blushed good for a straight-laced widow woman who wasn't at all interested in anything or anybody in his direction. So he picked up his glass and drifted over. He still thought Gaston was nuts, even though he understood and approved the game the sly old Frenchman was playing. Gaston grinned up at him and said, "Ah, there you are, you reluctant seducer of shy virgins. Allow me to present the Senoras Margo and Pilar, Ricardo mio. Last names are unimportant out at sea away from priests and other pests, so let us stay on familiar first-name terms, and Margo is with you."

Captain Gringo pulled up a bentwood chair and sat down to join them as he asked the younger one called Margo if she'd had a thing to say about that. She didn't answer. She just kept fluttering her fan like a sex-mad butterfly's wing, and though the plain golden ring on her fan-hand finger was sort of discouraging, she looked a lot prettier, up close, blushing so rosy.

That still wasn't saying a hell of a lot, however, since even flushed and smiling like Mona Lisa behind her black lace fan, old Margo had to be over forty; and from what he could see of her figure under the shapeless black gabardine two sizes too big for her, more than her face would have used a lift. But what the hell, they were no doubt just prick-teasing in the first place, and it would have hurt more had either one been worth drooling over.

Gaston was leaning close to the even older and uglier Pilar to whisper in her sort of withered ear as she gasped, giggled, and told him how awful he was. Captain Gringo didn't say anything much to Margo. If the dame didn't want to talk, she didn't want to talk, and as long as the other guys in the saloon thought he was trying to get laid, who cared? He'd been down this blind alley before. Most men had. The two silly dames would tease them until they got too tired or drunk to go on with it, and then they'd all get to say good-night, with a handshake, if he and Gaston were lucky. So he took out a claro, held it up for Margo to say yes or no, and when she shrugged and looked away, lit it. Gaston whispered something to Pilar, who gasped, slapped his elbow with her fan and said, "You should not say things like that, and besides, I have been married twice and know what you suggest is simply not at all possible!"

"Eh bien, how are you to know for certain unless we let me show you, mon cheri?"

"Oh, you terrible man! Do you know what he just told me, Margo?"

For the first time since he'd sat down with them, Captain Gringo heard Margo's voice, not a bad voice, sort of sultry, as she said, "I don't think I want to hear."

Pilar must have not believed her. She giggled and said, "He says his, ah, you know, is much longer than the cigar the one with *you* is smoking!"

Margo gasped and covered her face with her fan. Then she peered over the top of the black lace, thoughtfully, at the claro in Captain Gringo's teeth. Her eyes weren't bad. But then, what could be bad about bedroom eyes in almost any kind of a female face? He found himself blushing too, and this time *he* looked away. He noticed the guys across the saloon had stopped playing cards and were pretending not to watch as they watched with interest.

It got worse. The bartender came over with a tray of drinks—on the house, he said; and as he put them down by Captain Gringo, the jovial Jamaican whispered in English, "The boys are betting nine to five, Mon."

"For or against?" Captain Gringo sighed. But the bartender had moved away, so he had to figure it for himself. He figured the house was betting against him. He knew *he* would have. So he decided to end the charade one way or the other. He didn't give a damn, and it was getting silly. Whether the dames put out or slapped and ran was all the same to him, now that he and Gaston had established in front of plenty of witnesses that they were both normal sex maniacs. So he handed the drinks out, and then, as Margo took hers, he said, "Look, why don't we take these drinks to bed with us, Querida? It's getting late and people are starting to stare at us, so . . . ''

"Oh, Señor! Whatever are you suggesting?" She gasped.

So he said, "Look, it's simple. You're a woman. I'm a man. You're concave where I'm convex and neither of us are kids. So do you want to go on playing kid games, or do you want to got to bed with me, your place or mine?"

"Señor! I am not in the custom of allowing men to speak that way to me! You are, in fact, the first man who has ever dared to come right out and, *ask* for it like that!''

"Somehow I believe you." He grinned, starting to rise as he said, "Bueno, I can take a hint. I'll, ah, see you around the campus, Doll."

The last phrase had been said in English, partly because he wasn't sure if it made any sense in Spanish and partly because he didn't care if she understood. He muttered, "Good hunting. See you in the morning, early," to Gaston in the same language—as he made as graceful an exit as he could, wondering which of the guys across the room had just lost.

But as he stepped out on deck, Margo rose to follow him as, on the far side of the saloon, someone laughed and said, "Ole! That is fifty you owe me, Hernando!"

Captain Gringo stopped just outside, staring down bemused at the short dumpy figure who'd followed him out there. She licked her lips and asked, "Por favor, what was that last remark you made just now, Ricardo?"

He said, "The point gets lost in the translation. Your place or mine?"

"Oh, I could never go to a strange man's quarters. Only women of the lowest kind do that!"

"It's not a quarters, it's a stateroom. The rules are not the same in shipboard romances, see?"

"Es verdad? I confess I know little about such matters. Are you sure your neighbors . . . Oh, how silly of me, aboard a ship one *has* no neighbors, or at least no neighbors one is ever likely to meet in the marketplace, eh?"

"You're catching on fast. Let's go."

"Wait, I am still confused, Ricardo. You have not told me exactly for why we are going to this stateroom of yours. I mean, for to finish these drinks should only take a moment and then . . ."

"Oh hell, forget it," he growled, turning away as he added, "I'm going to bed. You can come with me or not. I don't give a damn either way, no offense."

He really didn't care if she followed him or not, so naturally she did, asking him why he was so angry. He sighed and said, "Look, Margo, if a guy wants to play kid games, he picks up a kid. I didn't just meet you hanging around a schoolyard with a brown paper bag in my hand, you know."

"Oh, that was such a cruel thing for to say, Ricardo. Do I really look that old to you?"

He didn't enjoy hurting women, even when they had it coming, so he stopped, turned to face her and said, "I never said you were *too* old, damn it. I just said we were both old enough to act like grown-ups. The names of the games is adultery, not infancy. If you're not adult enough, go play infancy with the boys in the bar some more."

He meant it. So of course she did no such thing. She told him he was horrid, and took his arm as they moved on to his own stateroom. He unlocked it and flipped the switch. Nothing happened. He muttered, "Bulb must be burned out. Make yourself at home while I replace it. They left some spares in this closet, if I can find this closet and...yeah, here we go."

It only took him a few moments to reach up and replace the light bulb in the low ceiling fixture. So he was surprised but not at all upset to discover, when the bulb suddenly flashed on in his upraised fingers, that Margo had made herself at home indeed, and fast. She smiled up coyly from the bunk, still holding her dumb fan to her face instead of the more important features now exposed by her stark-naked condition atop the bedcovers. She asked, coyly, if he was still interested in adult games. He said he sure was, and didn't waste much time shucking his own duds. But as he rolled onto the bunk naked with her and took her surprisingly youthful body in his arms, she tapped his nose with her fan and protested, "Wait, you said we could make love in the most adult worldly way, Ricardo!"

His old organ-grinder was stiff as a poker between them now, as it forgave her somewhat shopworn face and trembled to get inside her flawless torso, more so. He had to put it in her *some* damned where before he wasted a wad in midair; and, what the hell, he'd been the one who started the crap about sophisticated lovemaking. So to be a good sport, he asked her just what she had in mind, hoping she was as clean as she smelled and consoling himself with the thought that her snatch couldn't be any older than her middle-aged face, if a guy really had to kiss either one.

She said firmly, "You must lie flat upon your back and let me enjoy it my way first, por favor. After you have allowed me for to climax, I do not care what you do to me for your own enjoyment. For it has been, oh, Madre de Dios, so long since I have last made love *my* way to a man!"

He shrugged and lay back, assuming she was going to want to go sixty-nine for openers, but, what the hell, once a guy got used to the smell he had it half licked; and he was so hot right now it seemed only common courtesy and...Jeee-zusss! How was she doing that? Had she taken her damned *teeth* out behind that fan?

She had. There was no other answer, because no woman could have given such a great blow-job with even one tooth in her mouth! He stared at the overhead light, trying not to laugh as her head bobbed up and down. For in one way it seemed disgusting, or he knew it *should* have felt disgusting, to feel naked gums sliding up and down his moist erection, gripping tight as she rolled her wet tongue all over the head. But it didn't feel disgusting. It felt the way a blow-job was supposed to feel and often didn't. It felt as though she had a real cunt in her face. So, without further ado, he came in her mouth with a hiss of pure animal pleasure. Then he groaned that he was sorry he'd lost control but that he'd make it up for her if only she'd stop sucking and let him do it *right* for Chrissake.

She didn't stop sucking. If anything, she was abusing his confused shaft even more wildly, and so, though it should have been at least a little softer right now, she was holding its full attention as she Eskimo-kissed her nose back and forth in his pubic hair with her throat muscles contracting around the throbbing head as he gasped, "Jesus, have mercy, Margo! I don't want to come that way again. Let's save some ammunition for the main event!"

She answered with a moan from somewhere deeper in her throat as she swallowed the full length of his now fully aroused shaft as deep as it would go, with her lips pursed tightly around its roots and the base of her tongue wetly jerking him off while her throat muscles clamped tighter and tighter around his throbbing glans until, of course, he came that way again, even harder; and so, though he really had nothing to complain about, he growled, "This is crazy, Querida. What the hell are you supposed to be getting out of this?"

She swallowed, relaxed inside and slowly slid her still tightly pursed lips up and off his now semi-sated shaft with a sigh of vast contentment. Then she wiped her mouth with the back of her hand, kissed the head of his dong fondly and said, "Oh, that felt lovely. Could you not tell *I* was coming too, Ricardo?"

He propped himself up on one elbow to frown in confusion at her as he asked, "For Pete's sake, *how?* Were you playing with your own clit or something just now?"

She said, "I don't have to. It is a feeling that ends up down there, but it begins in my *throat,* see?"

"I don't see how that could work. But it must, if weird little guys hanging around public restrooms know what they're doing. I'll be damned if I've ever been able to figure cocksucking out. But come to think of it, how would I be able to?"

He laughed wryly as he thought back to the uneasy conversation he'd had earlier that same evening with the late Señorito Romero. But then he sobered as quickly, because it wasn't really funny to toss people overboard and because Margo was looking hurt as she sat upright beside him, holding that dumb fan in front of her face again. He said, "I'm not laughing at you. I'm laughing at me. You've got me sort of confused, Querida. You see, I'm usually the one who does all the work and . . . No shit, can you really come with your throat?"

She smiled down at him, with her teeth back in again—thanks to her fandango flutterings with that otherwise pointless fan—and then she replied, "I just did. Would you like for to fuck me now? I am most grateful for the way you indulged my *real* lusts, Ricardo."

He grinned and said, "*This* I gotta *see!*" Although, in truth, he really had feelings more than sights in mind. But the view was sort of inspiring too, as without further ado, Margo lay back and spread her shapely pale thighs in welcome as he rolled up on his hands and knees to crawl

into position above her. Her face was still only so-so, even
with her false teeth back in place; but she wasn't really
ugly, and from the neck down she was really beautiful.

He lowered his larger body down against her shapely
torso and noted how her firm ivory breasts seemed to fit
just right between them as he reached down and fumbled
his semi-erection in position to enter her right, for the first
time. It wasn't easy. Even if he'd been fully erect, Margo
had a surprisingly tight snatch for a lady with gray streaks
in her hair, all over.

She braced her bare heels against the mattress and thrust
her pelvis up at a more helpful angle as, at the same time,
she wrapped her soft, smooth arms up around him and
pulled him closer for what was, come to think of it, their
very first kiss.

That did it. The mingled feelings of desire and revulsion
sprang his bemused virile member almost fully erect again
as he couldn't help wondering what it would feel like to
kiss her with her false teeth out; if she'd take them out if
he asked; and why on earth a guy would want to *ask* such
a thing of a nice old lady!

He didn't. It seemed less important as he slowly worked
it into her vagina far enough to, yeah, thrust it in deep
enough to stay put, and, oh yes, her real thing was even
better than he'd expected!

But as he started to move in her, Margo just seemed to
be taking it, with neither reluctance nor enthusiasm. He
stopped—leaving it in, of course—to ask, "Would some
aspirin powders help? I think I have some in my kit bag
under the bunk."

She sighed and said, "I am *trying* for to respond to you
this way, Ricardo. Just do it. Do not worry about trying for
to please me this way. I assure you I do not mind."

"Oh gee, thanks. It really inspires a guy to hear the lady
he's laying couldn't care less, either way."

"Do not be angry, Ricardo. It is not my fault, any more
than it is your own, eh? I like you very much. I wish to
give you as much pleasure as you just gave me. So go
ahead and come in me this way. I *wish* for you to come in
me this way."

"Just for old time's sake, eh? I think we'd better talk about this, Margo. I don't usually like to discuss a lady's past with her while I'm getting to be part of it, but, no shit, you did say you were *married* one time, didn't you?"

"Si, my late husband never knew. It would have been cruel to tell him I felt nothing at all when he made love to me *this* way. He was much older than me, most old-fashioned in every way, and he just would not have understood."

"You're probably right. *I* sure don't! How the hell did you find out you really like oral sex better? Friendly neighbors?"

"Oh no, my husband would have killed me! I have never, never made love to anyone else while my husband lived, and oh, Ricardo, it took him ever so long for to die!"

"You both must have been relieved. But, okay, if you didn't take your late husband in the head and you didn't have a lover on the side, where did you find out you were a born sucker-offer?"

She sighed and said, "It is a long story, and you would not understand, Ricardo."

"Try me. I'm a naturally curious guy, and, hell, I really want to understand you better, Margo."

"I like you very much, too. But if you do not intend for to fuck me, and you do not seem to be doing so right now, would you like to take it out now?"

He thrust deeper and shook his head as he said, "It feels fine where it is. Who broke you in the other way?"

She covered her face with her dumb fan again as she murmured, "I swore never to tell. But *he* has been dead, too, for many years, and, oh Ricardo, how was I to know at the age of twelve what a sin we were committing in the eyes of the church?"

He grimaced and said, "Oboy, are we talking about playing doctor with the boy next door or the usual older friend of the family?"

She giggled, blushed and asked, "What do you know about seducing the daughters of your friends, Ricardo?"

He said, "Not much. I don't shoot fish in a barrel,

either. But you'd be surprised how many girls tell the same story about dear old Uncle Juaquin.''

She sighed and said, ''In this case it was a padre, not a tio. Not my real father, of course; my father confessor, at the church down the calle. You see, I confessed to him one day that I had learned how for to play with myself and that I could not stop no matter how many Hail Marias I said, so . . .''

''So, right, the saintly old pervert warned you little girls could go bananas playing with themselves and that if you couldn't stop masturbating, it was his Christian duty to show you the light. Did he lay you, too?''

''Oh heavens, no! As he explained, that would have been a sin for a celebate priest, so—''

''I get the picture,'' he cut in, utterly disgusted with a man he'd never know and would never get to punch out, now. He said, ''I don't know all that much about that psycho-whatever those docs in Vienna have been talking about lately, but I can see how a shy, confused and sexually excited young virgin could come almost any way with a grown man's wanger. So what happened after you got to sucking off at Confession a lot, Margo?''

She shrugged (it made her nipples tickle his chest), and said, ''I grew up and got married, of course. It was the custom in our village for a girl's parents to tell her who she should marry. My late husband was not a bad man. I could have done worse. But he would not have understood my true desires, and so, until just now—''

''Aw, come on!'' he cut in with a snort of disbelief, adding; ''No offense, but you haven't been twelve for some time, Margo. Are you trying to tell me you haven't had an orgasm once, in all this time?''

She giggled again and said, ''Well, a woman with needs does have ways to relieve herself. My late husband liked sausage. So he never questioned why we had it so often.''

Captain Gringo didn't want to even think about how a hard-up cocksucker masturbated with a sausage; and since, meanwhile, his curiosity was satisfied and his own cock wasn't, he started moving in Margo again. She asked blankly, ''Oh, do you still wish to do that, Ricardo?''

He growled, "I don't. It does. If I had any self-respect I'd take it out. But the little basser will never forgive me if I let anything built as nice as you between the thighs get off easy!"

She giggled again and even moved her hips a bit to help him as she said, "Oh well, in that case hurry up and come in me down there, Querido. We would not wish for your delicioso virile member to go away angry, eh?"

Captain Gringo grinned wryly and got down to business, consoling himself with the thought that at least he didn't have to worry about *waiting* for a sex partner who wasn't about to catch up no matter what he did. Her passive acceptance of what probably felt, at most, like a friendly back rub made it harder than usual to move with real inspiration or to even keep it hard as usual. He wondered, as what he was doing began to feel more like work than pleasure, what the hell he was *doing*. He didn't have to prove anything to her. He knew she didn't *give* a damn about what he was doing. He'd already enjoyed two damned fine orgasms with a dame he barely knew and would probably never see again. So was it really important that he finished in her right?

He decided it was, every time he paused for breath and debated just rolling off and forgetting the whole deal. He was starting to sweat. He was getting winded. He was sure he was going to climax in her any minute now, but it seemed every time he got up to the edge, the goddamn feeling faded and he had to start all over. His common sense kept telling him to quit. His glands kept promising him they'd let him, if only they could have her *this* way one lousy little time.

Margo must have noticed he was taking longer than any man should have, or probably ever had, in such a nice and tight little body. She said, "Heavens, you must like me more than I thought, Querido! You are so big, so strong and so passionate!"

"Sorry about that. I hope I'm not hurting you?"

"Not really. I told you I do not mind it this way. But I do wish you would hurry and come, por favor, for in truth it is starting to feel . . . strange. Does it help for me to move my hips more, like so?"

"It doesn't hurt. Could you, ah, sort of clamp down a little more, inside?"

"I don't know how, Ricardo."

"Sure you do. Just pretend you've just gone to the toilet, and tighten everything between your legs up the way you do when . . . Yeah, that's it. Thanks. It really helps."

She gasped, "Oh, you feel so *big* in me this way! But I can not keep it tight. I must let go and, grasp you again, and again, and, oh Ricardo! What is happeninggggggg?"

He asked her what she thought was happening as he started to really let himself go, sure he was almost there for sure, at last. But the son-of-a-bitching shaft seemed to hang-fire forever as he pounded as hard and fast as he could, so Margo, for the first time in her not-at-all-short life, experienced her very first vaginal orgasm; and if they didn't hear it up on the bridge, they just weren't listening.

He ejaculated in her orgasmic pulsations, fell limp atop her and gasped, "Jesus, keep it down to a roar! The whole ship will know what we're doing in here if you *scream* every time you come!"

She moaned, "I do not care! I do not care if the Pope in Rome hears I have just fucked, all the way, with my pussy at last!"

He rolled off, fumbled for his shirt and got out a claro and some matches to enjoy a smoke while they either got their second winds or decided to fall asleep and the hell with it. But sleep was the last thing Margo had in mind right now, and she didn't seem to want to wait for her second wind. So as Captain Gringo lay on his back with his head on the pillow, blowing smoke rings at the low overhead, Margo forked a shapely thigh across him and settled down to screw on top. It took some effort on her part to get it back in—after all it had already been in—but she was a persistent little thing and she looked so yummy, squirming around up there above him, that he was able to rise to the occasion enough, as long as she was willing to do all the work.

Neither of them would have enjoyed their protracted orgy as much, that night, had they been privy to a conversation that was taking place on the bridge above them at the same time. The old Scotch skipper didn't allow talking on the bridge unless it was important. So even the Cuban helmsman at the wheel was listening with interest as the mate said, "That Costa Rican fairy's not in his bunk after all, Sir. I jimmied one of the slats in the door vent as you ordered, and despite the Don't Disturb, his stateroom's empty!"

The skipper nodded and said, "Ay, I knew something was up when the deck watch didna' hear a peep out of the wee beastie all this time. For if there's one thing I ken about screaming faggots, it's that they scream overmuch in bed wi' man or beast. Where do you mind the queer-legged creature can be if he's not in his bunk?"

The mate said, "Well, if he's not overboard he has to be shacked up somewhere else on the ship, Skipper."

"Och, tell me something I dinna ken, Mon! They say Romero was buttering up to that tall blond Yank earlier this nicht. Ye've checked *his* door vents out, of course?"

The mate chuckled and replied, "Ay ay, Sir, and if there's one thing that banana broker is not, it's queer. You know those two Costa Rican widows who've steamed up and down the coast with us before?"

"Ay, but they've never been ones for mucking with the men on board. So don't tell me either's with that big Yank young enough to be their wee bairn!"

The mate laughed outright this time and said, "I just did, Sir. I couldn't tell whether the old bag was fucking him or giving birth to him just now, but he was in her box one way or another, and she sure looks different with her duds off!"

The skipper allowed himself a frosty smile as he said, "Wonders never cease along the Mosquito Coast. Which sister puts out?"

"*Both* of them, Skipper. That little Frenchman calling himself 'Fontleroy' was with the *older* sister when I peeked through the slats just now, and that was *really* comical! It seems to be true what they say about Frenchmen, but, Jesus, she's so old and ugly!''

The skipper grimaced and said, "At least the wee froggy's with a *female* of the species. So we can forget about at least *four* of the passengers. But that wee fruitie Romero has to be with at least one other, damn it, and if it's one thing I won't stand for on this vessel it's out-and-out sodomy. So get back to work and find out whose bunk Romero's snuck into, damn it.''

The mate shrugged and answered, "I'm running out of places to look, Sir. He doesn't seem to be with any of the other passengers, and if he was up in the fo'ci'sle I'd have heard about it by now. It's hard to keep news of a gangbang on board from getting around when the crew doesn't have private bunks—''

"Och, I'll have no talk of the *crew* involved with yon faggot even if they are!" the skipper cut in, adding; "Romero's nae worth the powder to blow him to fairyland, but his family is too important for a wee steamship line to cross! Gae look for him some more. He may be in one of the lifeboats looking for the soap, or, och, even doon in the hold making someone happy among the cargo cases. But make sure he's still *aboard,* and report back to me as soon as ye do.''

"And if he's *not* on board at all, Sir?''

"We'll just have to turn someone in for pushing him overboard, of course. We canna have the damned police in any port poking about for wee clues aboard this ship, Mister. The trouble with police is that they sometimes poke their noses into places a businessmon in our line of business may nae want 'em *poking*! Och, must I draw ye a picture, Mon? Ye ken as well as me our bills of lading don't always match the cargo we unlade hither and yon too closely.''

The mate smiled thinly and said, "That's for sure, Skipper. But how are we to hang a missing pansy on one of the other passengers if they're all behaving themselves in their own quarters right now?''

The skipper sighed and muttered, "Och, the daft lad *does* need pictures on the chalkboard! Did ye nae just tell

me all our passengers are *alone,* separately, or at least no
more than two to a stateroom at the moment?''

"Yessir, and none of them are with the missing pansy."

"Och, Laddy, Laddy, who's to say whether that could
be true or nae? Do we look like men who peek through
vents at nicht? We'll be putting into Mission Bay in the
morning. Give the wee Romano till then to turn up. If he
hasn't we'll report him missing to the British constabulary
there.''

"But won't that mean a full investigation team of
British lawmen coming aboard, Sir?''

"It would if we couldn't tell them who we saw push the
wee fairy over the side, Mon. But why should even a
colonial copper muck about in a stuffy hot hold when he's
been told by honest ship's officers who to arrest for the
dark deed?''

The mate nodded and said, "That ought to work,
Skipper. But who do we have in mind as the guilty
party?''

The skipper shrugged and said, "I'll think about it.
Let's hope Romero's just misbehaving somewhere aboard
for now. If he's still missing when we reach Mission Bay,
we'll just have to hand it on anyone who fits, as long as he
nae a member of the crew.''

Captain Gringo woke up when he heard some idiot
gonging the breakfast chimes outside. He was alone in a
very rumpled bed. He didn't care. Before slipping out
discreetly before dawn, Margo had screwed him sillier
than lots of lots of better-looking dames had ever managed
to. As experienced travelers up and down the Mosquito
Coast, he and Gaston had naturally booked seaward-facing
staterooms, to avoid the furnace glare of the afternoon sun
above the shoreline to the west. The only trouble with that
was how the morning sun, which wasn't that much cooler
in the tropics, glared in through the ventilating slats and
painted everything inside with tiger stripes of purple shade

and glare that was too bright to look at with sleep-gummed eyes. So he rubbed his eyes, got up and staggered to the corner washstand to wash, with a tepid washrag, his face and everything else Margo had slobbered over. He really did have some of the new aspirin powders under the bunk, and his head felt as though it were full of belly-button fuzz. But he wasn't really hurting, and by the time you futsed around getting the white powder out of its little waxed-paper envelope into a glass of water, any headache a guy might have could be gone. He settled for brushing his teeth instead.

Then he shaved, wiped himself all over once for luck with the wet rag and got dressed for breakfast. He met Gaston out on deck. For some reason the little Frenchman looked as if he could have used some aspirin powders, too. Captain Gringo said, "I just had a funny idea. You know those new headache powders the Bayer Company puts out? What if they made them up as pills instead of loose aspirin-powder packets? Wouldn't that be a handier way to get the stuff down in a hurry? I wonder if a guy could patent an idea like that."

Gaston grimaced and replied, "Someone may, someday, but it won't be you or me, my disgustingly awake and inventive. To apply for a patent, one needs a permanent address; and when one has as many people interested one's present whereabouts as you or me, ooh la la! How did you make out with the shy one last night?"

"She's not as shy these days. Please don't tell me what a great lay yours was, Gaston. Right now, just the thought of pussy makes me feel like going back to sleep."

"I need ham and eggs more than codfish pie at the moment, too. But what do we say to them over the breakfast table, hein?"

"It's lady's choice, of course. If they don't know us, we don't know them, see?"

"Merde alors, that part's easy. What if they wish to make the eyes goo-goo avec amour at us in front of the other passengers?"

Captain Gringo repressed a shudder and said, "It's the chance a guy just has to take when he leaps on any dame's bones. I know we all do it anyway, but a guy shouldn't ever kiss a dame in private that he'd be ashamed to be seen with in public."

"Easy for you to say." Gaston sighed, going on to explain, "I took Pilar to bed in hopes she might at least have a decent body under that shapeless black dress. Alas, the loose clothing flattered her très ridicule. It took all my pride in the honor of France to continue, once I saw how ugly she was all over!"

"But you managed, right?"

"But of course. Would you want a seedy old Costa Rican widow spreading word all over Latin America that Frenchmen were impotent?"

Since by now they'd reached the dining room, Captain Gringo didn't have to answer that. Inside, the skipper had already taken his place at the head of his table, and better yet, the other seats were filled with earlier risers, including the two sisters. So the two soldiers of fortune sat down gratefully at another table; and though there were neither ham nor eggs on the menu, they managed. They ate fast and got out and over to the main saloon, where there were more empty chairs. They ordered tall drinks to nurse and carried them to the now empty corner the card game had been held in the night before. The table was still there. So they spread their highball glasses and ashtray on it and settled back to wait for the boat to get somewhere more interesting.

Neither Margo nor Pilar came in, but the skipper and first mate did. The bellied up to the bar together and seemed to be having a serious discussion with the Hispanic bartender now on duty. For a guy with a drinker's nose, the skipper sure seemed to take his time deciding what to order.

Another male passenger came in from the promenade, spotted the two English-speaking soldiers of fortune in the corner and came to join them. He sat down at the table uninvited, an insult that could get a stranger killed in many a Spanish-speaking cantina. But the dumb shit didn't look Hispanic, so what the hell.

He introduced himself as D. C. Dodd, the Reverend D. C.

Dodd, without going into just what hell-fire-and-damnation Calvinist sect he revved for. He said, "I hope I have fallen among Christian gentlemen, for the Devil has me over the barrel and, Lord have mercy, I just don't know what I'll do if you boys of my own faith and color let a fellow Christian down!"

"How much?" asked Gaston, followed by Captain Gringo asking, "Better yet, how come? Didn't I see you playing cards at this very table last night, Rev?"

Dodd stared sheepishly down at the empty space in front of his uninvited space at the table and licked his lips wistfully as the two soldiers of fortune sized him up. They didn't have to exchange comments. For once they were in complete agreement, and each knew what the other had to be thinking. The Reverend Dodd looked more like a beachcomber in a stolen clean outfit he hadn't shit in yet than a man of the cloth, or come to think of it, a man. He was a flabby middle-aged guy of average height who looked like a tough ten-year-old could whip him. His pallid face was spiderwebbed with the little red lines of too much steady booze. But everywhere a blood vessel hadn't burst, his complexion looked more like unbaked piecrust. He'd have probably been even paler if he hadn't been in the tropics. He swallowed air instead of the drink he wanted, and said, "I said I'd been tricked by the Devil, I say the *Devil*, Son! Those greasers who forced me into a game of chance last night were in league, I say in *league*, against me.!"

"In other words, you're tapped out?"

"That's about the size of it, Son. I'm so ashamed I could kill myself if suicide wasn't an even more serious sin than playing cards. But life must go on, so if you could stake me to enough to get by on till we reach Limon, I'd be proud, I say *proud*, to pay you back there. You see, I'm a missionary for the Reformed True Baptist Church, and as soon as I can cable my congregation for more funds—"

"No soap," Captain Gringo cut in, with a polite but cynical smile. He said, "You may or may not be a Hard-Shell Baptist preacher. But you're full of shit."

Dodd looked hurt and replied, "Them's hard, I say

hard, words, Son! If I wasn't a man of the cloth, I'd ask for satisfaction on the field of honor from a man who as much as called me a liar!''

Captain Gringo shrugged and said, ''It's a good thing your religion doesn't allow you to fight, then. What does it say in your charter about playing cards with strangers on steamboats, Rev?''

''I just allowed, I say *allowed*, I *sinned* last night, blast it! I sinned worse than playing cards! I allowed the demon rum to pass between my lips, and that was the beginning of my downfall as it ever is with mortal flesh! I'm sure those spicks put something in the rum punch they offered me after supper. They said it was a harmless refreshment made with more fruit juice than liquor, but the next thing I knew I was seated at this very table, letting them teach me a game of chance they called Picar Americano, I think.''

''It was stud poker, and you were dealing pretty good,'' said Captain Gringo with a disgusted look. Before Dodd could answer, Gaston nudged him and murmured, ''Regard, the skipper seems to be talking about us at the bar. I just caught his eye in the mirror and he quickly looked away, très *guilty!*''

Captain Gringo shrugged and said, ''Let him look all he likes. We're not playing stud with this flimflam artist.''

Dodd gasped and insisted, ''Damn it, I say damn it and *double* damn it, I'm a man of the cloth; and if you're so smart, tell me how come I was the one who *lost* last night?''

''How do we know you did? We weren't around when the game ended.''

''Lord have mercy, are you accusing me of asking for help under false, I say *false*, colors, Son?''

''It's what you're doing, isn't it? Your tale of woe won't wash, Rev. Whether you took those other guys last night or they took you, you're a passenger aboard a half-ass passenger vessel. Three meals a day come with the ticket you had to buy to board her, right?''

''Yes, but a man has other needs, and, honestly, Son, I don't have the wherewithal on me to buy myself an after-dinner cigar!''

"You mean a drink, and you're still full of shit, Rev. You know you could charge all the booze and tobacco that would be good for your health and settle up with the purser in Limon."

"Damn it, I say *damn* it, I just spoke to the purser about a line of credit, and he turned me down flat, the papist rascal!"

Captain Gringo took a sip of his own drink before he observed, "He must know you better than we do, then. You must be a poor tipper as well as a loser, Rev. Any purser worth his salt would be able to cable home for you at any of the ports this tub will hit before it ever hits Limon. So if he said no, he knows as well as we do that there just won't be any money from home waiting for you in Limon."

Dodd looked downcast and said, "All right, you've got me cold: and you're right, I say you're *right,* that I'm a poor wayfaring stranger without two coins to rub together and no way in the world of ever paying your kindness back. But you look like a couple of real kind gents, so how much kindness can I hope for?"

Gaston, to Captain Gringo's mild surprise, started to reach in his pants. But the younger American kicked his ankle to stop him as he told Dodd flatly, "Nothing. Zero. Goose eggs. I'd stake anyone I wasn't mad at to a warm meal and flop, Rev. But you're booked into a stateroom as good as mine; and like I said, they serve three meals a day to all passengers. So you've got your meals and your flop, and I don't buy booze or poker chips for bums."

Dodd tried to brazen it out with, "What happens when we get to Limon, I say Limon? Honestly, Son, I'm flat busted and don't know a soul there!"

"Tough titty. We never told you to go there. So go somewhere else, Dodd. You're starting to steam me. I mean it."

"Good Lord, would you threaten a man of the cloth?"

"I'm not threatening you. I'm telling you. If you're a Baptist missionary, I'm a Catholic nun. So take a hike. I'm not going to say it again."

Dodd rose, muttering something most unchristian under

his breath, and moved over to the bar. Gaston chuckled dryly and said, "Sacre bleu, did we have to be so hard on the poor species of insect, Dick?"

Captain Gringo said, "Not if we weren't putting into a place to get off any minute. Did you really want that pest tagging along after a couple of soft touches?"

"Ah, I stand corrected and, merde alors, regard what the lying cochon is up to at this very moment!"

Captain Gringo shot a weary glance at the bar and said, "I told you so," as the desperately broke Reverend Dodd lit a Havana perfecto, Scotch and soda in hand. The skipper had left for the bridge or somewhere, but the mate was still there, a few spaces down from Dodd. As his eyes met those of Captain Gringo in the mirror behind the bar, the mate lifted his own glass in a silent toast and winked. Captain Gringo nodded back as he told Gaston, "I was right. Dodd works this steamer line regularly."

SS *Trinidad* steamed over the bar into the harbor of Mission Bay with the eleven-thirty tide. Everyone on board who didn't have a chore to work at naturally stood out on deck to watch the low, palm-fringed shoreline approach. Slow coastal voyages made people act like that. The crown colony of Mission Bay wasn't much to look at, but at least it was *something* to look at.

Like most seaports along the Mosquito Coast, the British outpost lay on dead-flat, not-too-solid ground. Inland, Nicaragua went up a lot more. Some of the more dramatic volcanic peaks even managed snowfields despite the latitude. But you couldn't tell it from the swampy lowlands. A brown sluggish river divided the British settlement—or rather two settlements—as it ran into the big but shallow bay that gave the place its name. One of the crewmen told one of the nearby passengers that the English had named the river—what else—the Mission River. Farther inland, the Nicaraguans no doubt called it something else, but what did *they* know? Like other coaling stations the Royal

Navy had carved out of the mangrove- and Indian-haunted coastal plain of Nicaragua back in the forties, this "little bit of England" was too far from the more settled parts of Nicaragua for even the Nicaraguans to do more than bitch about. They were usually too busy fighting with one another to take on the Royal Navy, in any case.

As they neared the cobblestone quay of the settlement to the north side of the river, it became clearer that this particular little part of England was working the cliché to the point of artsy-craftsy. A white church steeple that looked as if it had been designed by Christopher Wren dominated the skyline. It probably had been. Old Sir Christopher had been a whiz at running up new English Baroque churches, cheap, after the Great London Fire, and his plans had been copied by lots of church builders in New as well as Old England. This particular one looked sort of silly with palm and pepper trees sharing its space against a cobalt tropic sky.

The two soldiers of fortune were pleased to see they were going to tie up at the quay instead of dropping anchor out in the roads and unlading by lighter. Getting down a gangplank could be a lot less complicated than talking oneself into a bum-boat. They held back and kept to themselves as the vessel docked. Each had filled his pockets with stuff from his kit bag he just had to have— and left said kit bag plainly visible in his stateroom. Each, of course, wore his double-action .38 invisibly under a linen jacket—and was there any law saying a guy couldn't step out on deck with his mosquito boots and planter's sombrero on? So they were ready to move out, the moment they could. The moment they could would be the tricky part. They heard one of the other passengers ask the purser how long they'd have ashore, and the purser told the other leg-stretcher to forget it, explaining, "We're only dropping off a few cases of canned goods, and we won't be picking any cargo up here in Gilead. So there won't be time for shore leave."

The two soldiers of fortune exchanged puzzled glances. Gaston said not to ask him. The question was answered for them when the other passenger asked it and the mate explained, "The colony's called Mission Bay because it's lousy with do-gooders who came to do good and did right well for themselves. This settlement north of the river's called Gilead, after a town in the Good Book. The one down there to the south is called Zion. Same reason. The lime-juicers in Zion are even crazier. So there's no point in going ashore anyway. You can't get screwed, blewed or tatooed anywhere on Mission Bay."

Captain Gringo and Gaston weren't worried about getting screwed, blewed or tatooed. They just wanted to get off before someone got around to asking them what they knew about the late Hector Romero or, worse yet, where they'd gotten those fake passports and IDs that wouldn't stand up to close examination in good light. So they played it cool until the ship was tied up and the gangplank lowered for the skipper and some ship's officers to go down to the quay and argue with some other guys. The men waiting for whatever the ship was delivering didn't look nearly so British as the church steeple behind them. As Captain Gringo lounged at the rail with Gaston, he muttered, "If those guys are English, I'm an Eskimo."

Gaston shrugged and said, "They are très dusky, even for the cast of Spanish types one usually finds in charge down here. But what of it? The Anglo-Saxon prefers darker meat to do his work of dirtiness, non?"

"Yeah, but you'd think the guys taking delivery in a British port would be lighter, and wearing snappier outfits. Those guys look like native stevedores."

"Oui, and regard that net filled avec crates our jolly vessel seems to be swinging ashore for them. Perhaps they *are* stevedores, non?"

"Non. You don't just dump a cargo on the docks without some guy in a suit and tie signing for it. There ought to be customs inspectors around here, too. Have you ever been in a For-Chrissake-British crown colony where a ship can just steam in and unlade without at least one guy in a pith helmet glancing at your bill of lading?"

"Mais non. On the other hand, our droll species of skipper seems to be some species of Scotchman; and we have been flying the British Merchant colors for some time, hein? Perhaps they put in here on a regular basis and the local authorities would just as soon not act so stuffy under a noonday sun.''

Captain Gringo shook his head and said, ''Brits *always* act stuffy under a noonday sun. That's one reason they run India these days instead of the people who grew up there. There's something funny going on around here. Are you sure this is the last port of call before Limon?''

''Mais non, do I look like I run this species of tub, Dick? They may or may not stop somewhere further down the coast before it is too late for us to make a graceful exit. But do we want to chance it?''

''Not really. They should have already missed Romero by now, and the one nice thing about a port run so sloppy is that guys who'll let a steamer drop off cargo without formalities are hardly likely to ask a couple of guys buying drinks for some ID! There's nobody by the gangplank now. Let's go for it!''

They did. They simply moved to the gangplank and were halfway down it before a voice that sounded like a schoolroom tattle-tale called after them, ''We're not supposed to go ashore! The purser will be angry!''

They ignored the other passenger. Guys like that were usually safe to ignore. Captain Gringo in the lead steered around a pile of freshly unloaded crates with the skipper on the far side talking to the natives with his back to the pile. One of the other ship's officers spotted them, frowned, but simply took out his pocket watch and held up two fingers. He probably meant two hours, since two minutes seemed silly.

There was usually a line of shabby cantinas facing a waterfront, but they didn't see anything like that open or, in fact, anything like that at all. There was a ship's chandler, a sail loft and a boarded-up barbershop facing them as they made it across the quay to the shade. Captain Gringo said, ''This way,'' and led Gaston to the first slot in the storefronts he spotted. Gaston said, ''I wonder where that one who saw us thinks we are going.'' So Captain Gringo stopped and eased back to the corner to have a peek around it, back the way they'd just come. The men off SS *Trinidad* weren't looking his way. He said, "If they noticed at all, they may think we have to take a leak." then he added, "Oh, shit! Look out there on the water, just ahead of the steamer's bows!"

Gaston did. He saw the same little steam launch flying the same officiously large British flag from its stern as it chugged its way their way. So they agreed they'd better get away from the waterfront, poco tiempo, because more than one jerk-off over that way knew they were ashore and which way they'd just gone!

It was Gaston who suggested a haunted house, or at least an empty house to haunt until the SS *Trinidad* was out of the harbor and their hair. Captain Gringo agreed there had to be some empty buildings of some kind somewhere around here. Thanks to the raw materials boom of the 1880s, most tropic ports tended to be overbuilt. A lot of get-rich-quickers had gone broke in the worldwide financial panic of '87, and a bankrupt banana or sugar firm could hardly take its warehouse with it as it went out of business. So as they moved inland along the tree-shaded red clay streets of Gilead, he started looking for places that looked deserted.

There was an embarrassment of riches. More than half the places they passed looked as if nobody had been home in some time. Such business structures as there might be in the little town were closer to the waterfront and the housing they were passing now looked residential. But where were the residents? As usual in an English-speaking colony, the little houses on either side had been built in the bungalow style the Brits had invented in India as a half-ass compromise between an Englishman's Castle and a place more suited to the tropics. Little picket-fenced dooryards had been planted to look as much like English country gardens as one could manage with the lusher vegetation that grew down this way. Even a lime-juicer who dressed for dinner and insisted on roast beef with the temperature in the nineties knew that if you planted an apple tree south of the Tropic of Cancer, you got one hell of a big apple tree and no apples. So the lemon and mango in the yards made sense. But the way the weeds were growing behind the sun-bleached pickets didn't. He said, "Jesus, I don't think anyone's mowed their lawn for at least a couple of months, anywhere on this block."

Gaston said, "Oui, the colonial Englishman is a fiend for whitewash when he does not have to apply it himself, and regard how much wood is showing through along that veranda across the street. Shall we drop in and ask if the property is for rent? I do not think I wish to *buy* such a run-down property, hein?"

Captain Gringo hesitated, then said, "Right. If we're wrong and there's someone there, we can say ... what? That we're selling magazine subscriptions?"

"Let me do the talking. I shall ask directions in French. I have yet to meet a middle-class English housewife who speaks French."

They had to go somewhere. So Captain Gringo opened the gate, noting how rusty its hinges were, and they waded through the waist-high weeds to the front steps. As Gaston knocked on the peeling green paint of the front door, Captain Gringo moved to a dusty window, peered in and said, "Empty. Not even a stick of furniture inside."

So Gaston took out his pocketknife to pick the lock but when he found the door unlocked, he simply opened it and they stepped inside.

The place smelled moldy. That was because it was. Unless one kept at it in the tropics, woodwork began to mold and rot in no time. Gaston said, "I wonder if they left anything to eat or, better yet, to drink." But Captain Gringo told him to stay put as he moved to the nearest shadeless dusty window and peered out through the grime to see if anyone else in the neighborhood wanted to make anything out of their visit.

There didn't seem to be anyone else in the neighborhood. Not even a tree leaf was stirring in the fetid afternoon air as he stared out at the blank-eyed houses all around. He said, "This is weird. Where do you suppose everyone *went*, Gaston?"

The Frenchman shrugged and asked, "Who cares? Perhaps there was a crop failure, a plague or some other such jolly occurrence, hein?"

"People don't drop off cargo at a ghost town. Those natives taking delivery back there looked pretty solid, too. Let's look around."

They did, but the empty house had little to say to them. The people who'd once lived there had moved out neatly, not even leaving a mess behind them. So the evacuation had been planned and unhurried. The wallpaper was starting to peel in places and sprout moss in others, but there no sign of a fire, a struggle or any other sudden emergency. They'd just moved away, period.

There was no upstairs to explore. So Captain Gringo told Gaston, "We need a higher vantage point, and it doesn't look like those are as hard to find in Gilead as I thought they might be. Let's see if we can find a taller house to haunt. I'd like to know what that steamer's doing about now."

Gaston said he was sort of interested, too. So they went out the back door, crossed more weeds and worked their way along an alley that was starting to revert to jungle. Just for the hell of it, they tried a couple of other houses farther down the way. They were deserted, too. Captain Gringo muttered, "Shit, those guys who met the ship must live *some* damned where!" and Gaston said, "Oui, but most likely in the usual native quarter. You English do not like dusky neighbors. So, most naturally, natives who work for you live on the other side of les tracks, non?"

"Watch your mouth. I'm Connecticut Yankee, not English, and I doubt if there are any tracks running through this neck of the woods. Where the hell would a railroad run to?"

"Ah, oui, from time to time, when they are not having a civil war, the Nicaraguans do seem to think this neck of les woods is theirs. Never the less, we shall find a native quarter across some sort of established boundary line. Perhaps the drag of main? There were hardly enough business establishments near the waterfront for even a town of these modest proportions, hein?''

They came out of the alley. Across a green—now overgrown knee-deep in freshly self-sewn sea grape—stood the white frame church they'd noticed from the sea. It's whitewash was in bad shape, too, and a side door gaped open on its hinges. Captain Gringo grinned and said, "Perfect. We'll have a bird's-eye view of the whole layout from up in the belfry." He paid no attention when Gaston asked if he didn't mean a bat's-eye view. The church did look a little spooky inside, although not so run-down and decayed as the other places they'd just explored. The church had probably stayed in business longer as the other colonists abandoned ship, for whatever reason. He led the way down a side aisle, found the door to the belfry—or at least a door leading to a ladder running straight up—and said, "This ought to be the way up into the steeple. Let's go."

Gaston followed, albeit bitching all the way. Captain Gringo shoved the trapdoor at the top of the ladder out of the way and helped Gaston up into the belfry. The bells were still there. So was a thick crunchy layer of moss-covered guano. He told Gaston, "When you're right, you're right. This is bat shit, sure as hell. Remember that cave in Mexico?''

"Only too vividly! Let us depart before we catch rabies! Regard that mass of brown fur above us, you triple-headed idiot!''

Captain Gringo glanced up, gulped and said, "Hell, they're all asleep at this hour. They might not all be rabid, anyway.''

"Merde alors, *one* rabid bat will do it, and there must be more than a *thousand* hanging up there in the hollow of that steeple!''

Captain Gringo moved to the belfry shutters and peered out. He said, "Hot damn! I can see the steamer from here and, better yet, they're hauling in the gangplank!''

"I am still going to die of rabies, avec foaming at the mouth and biting you on your stubborn derriere! What of our jolly British harbor patrol?''

Captain Gringo didn't see *any* kind of watercraft moving out on the flat, calm waters of Mission Bay, although it was hard to make out distant detail at this time of day. The overhead sun was steaming a shimmering haze off both the harbor and surrounding tropic vegetation. He could see down the bay as far as the river pretty well. The other township of Zion was a sort of wavering blur. He couldn't tell if people or just the walls and rooftops were dancing in the sunlight like that. He turned around to rest his eyes in the bat-scented darkness of the belfry. He said, "I think we made it. We'll know soon enough." Then he hunkered down, took out a claro and lit up. Gaston, still on his feet, growled, "Merde alors, can't we get out of this bird cage filled with bats, now?"

Captain Gringo said, "Sure we can. We just have to go back down the ladder and hope we don't run into a shore party from the steamer. They know we came ashore. I don't see how they could have seen us get back aboard, so . . ."

Gaston hunkered down beside him, cursing in a mixture of French and Arabic, and got his own smoke going. The silently smoked their cigars short. Then Captain Gringo rose for another peek and said, "Thar she goes. But how come no thar she *blows*?"

"Dick, are you saying anything at all or just making noises? I thought my English was formidable until I met you. Explain your latest words of wisdom in less cryptic fashion, hein?"

Captain Gringo said, "When a steamer leaves port, she's supposed to sound off, even when she hasn't left at least two passengers stranded. The skipper didn't sound his siren coming in. He's leaving just as sneaky. How do you figure it?"

"Sacre goddamn, do I look like a skipper of steamships? Perhaps his tooter is simply broken. He put in by broad daylight. We saw a British harbor patrol launch puffing over for a chat with him about his visit. Perhaps they did not wish to wake up these rabid bats above us. Who else was there to toot at?"

"Us. They knew we'd come ashore. They should have

given us a warning blast on the siren before shoving off like that, damn it!''

Gaston laughed incredulously and said, "Merde alors, we go to so much trouble to desert the ship, and now you are angry because we got away with it?''

Captain Gringo chuckled sheepishly and said, "Yeah, we did, didn't we? Let's go back down and scout up some friendly natives. We'll just hole up here until another vessel going our way puts in, and that'll be that.''

The first native they met met them at the foot of the ladder and didn't really look too native. She was about nineteen, obviously Anglo-Saxon and obviously confused as hell to see them coming out of the ladder door. Her voice was as peppery as her red hair when she asked, "Who are you two, and what have you been up to in our belfry?''

Captain Gringo smiled down at her and said, "We thought this place was deserted, Miss, ah . . . ?''

"Perkins, Olivia Perkins, and I'm not a miss, I'm married to the Reverend Hiram Perkins; and you still haven't told me who you are or why I just caught you creeping about our church when it's not open for services!''

He introduced himself and Gaston, by the same phony names, as he regarded her trim figure wistfully. She was dressed in a modest-enough Gibson girl blouse and skirt, but old Gibson knew what he was doing when he put his yummies in that up-to-date summer outfit. There was no point in staring, though, if she was married. So to soothe her he explained, "We seem to have missed our ship. We climbed up in the belfry just now to see if we could spot it.''

"And did you?''

"I'm afraid so. Putting out to sea. I guess we're beached here until the next coastal vessel puts in. Would you have any notion when that might be, Ma'am?''

She frowned thoughtfully. She was pretty, no matter what she did with her soft but fine-boned features. She said, "Oh dear, you gentlemen may be beached indeed! Didn't anyone tell you this colony has been abandoned by the Crown?''

"You and your husband still seem to be here, Ma'am."

An odd look flickered across her face. Then she lowered her emerald green eyes and murmured, "So we are. You'd better talk to Hiram about it. He understands the situation better than I do. Or at least he *says* he does."

She turned away to lead them the length of the church, out the same side door and around to the rectory behind the larger building. The private quarters of the minister and his young wife were built in the same style. The rectory could have used a coat of whitewash, too, and the yard was going to reach up and strangle them all in their sleep if someone didn't get at it was a grass whip pretty soon. But it wouldn't have been polite to tell a lady she was a sloppy housekeeper; and as she led them in via the back door, they could see that the interior of the house, at least, was still in order.

Olivia sat them at her kitchen table and placed some tea and biscuits on it between them before going to fetch her husband. The tea was cold. The biscuits were stale. But it didn't take long for the redhead to return with a man old enough to be her father and then some. She introduced him as her husband, the Reverend Hiram Perkins. He creaked himself down to a seat at the head of the table, and when his wife poured tea for him, he said, gently but firmly, "Olivia, Dear, this tea has gone cold and flat."

She shrugged and said, "Don't drink it then. I've used all the firewood those lazy niggers left out back before they ran away to the jungle to eat people, damn it!"

"Olivia, Dear Heart, in front of *guests*?"

The redhead started to say something, flounced her head and stormed out of the room instead, leaving all three men staring at one another awkwardly.

Perkins sighed and said, "You must forgive her, gentlemen. She's rather upset at Her Majesty these days, and I fear she tends to lash out at those closer to her."

Captain Gringo nodded soberly and said, "We couldn't help noticing this town was sort of, ah, spooky, Sir. What's going on here in Gilead?"

Perkins tried another sip of Olivia's awful tea, put his cup back down with a grimace of distaste and said,

"Hardly anything at all, at the moment. As you see, only a few are left here. I don't know what's gotten into Whitehall, but they seem to have decided to return this colony to Nicaragua. Can't imagine what the perishing Nicaraguans want with it. No Nicaraguans living within fifty miles. But there you have it."

From the doorway, his wife spat, "It's all the work of that bloody Yank, Grover Cleveland! Who is the bloody President of the bloody States to tell freeborn English where they might or might not have a colony? Did Victoria Regina sign any bloody Monroe Doctrine? She did bloody not! Did even the perishing *Nicaraguans* sign the bloody Monroe Doctorine? Coo, the flaming dagos couldn't even *read* the bloody thing!"

Her husband sounded something like a bleating sheep as he begged her, "Olivia, please! Your *language,* Dear Heart!"

"Oh, bloody, bloody, bloody!" she replied, and then flounced out again. Some dames were like that when they didn't know just where they wanted to be. Old Hiram was doubtless trying to cover for her as he said, "She has a point, you know. It seems our Foreign Office has the wind up since that Venezuelan crisis a few months ago. You two must have heard about that of course?"

"Yeah, just a little," said a smiling Captian Gringo, who along with Gaston had actually taken part in a showdown that had almost led to a real no-kidding war between Great Britain and the United States.

The minister said, "I couldn't understand it at all myself. Until this Cleveland chap got himself elected, nobody though the so-called Monroe Doctrine applied to *us*! But with a maniac in Washington who really seems to mean what he says, London seems to want to smooth things over by playing up to the blighter for now. So, since this colony was acquired in a rather, ah, informal manner while the Dons were at one of their seasonal revolutions a few years ago—"

His wife cut in from the doorway again with, "Coo, are we giving back British Honduras with its mahogany? We are not! Are we letting those bloody bandito barstards have Bluefields with its pearl beds and sponge-flats back? Not bloody *likely!* They've sold us out because there's nothing here but souls to save, and the bloody barstards in Whitehall wouldn't know a soul if they woke in bed with one, for not one of them ever *had* a soul, the bloody sods!''

Then she lit out again. Captain Gringo couldn't help wondering where she went when she wasn't cussing from the doorway. As if he hadn't noticed, he told her husband, ''Well, whatever the reason, all the deserted dwellings we just passed are starting to make sense. But the ship we came in on just dropped off a lot of stuff, Sir. So there must be *some* people left here now, right?''

Before Perkins could answer, Olivia shouted in at them, ''Coo, there's nobody left on this side of the river but the bloody dagos, and half of *them's* run away! What are *we* staying here for, Husband? All the whites are across the river in Zion, and who knows how long *they'll* be there? The flaming game is up! They've sold us out to the bloody Nicks! Can't you see that?''

He must have heard, from the way he grimaced. But he answered Captain Gringo instead, sort of, by saying or asking, ''What else can we do? My church back home sent me here on a mission to the Indians, and they'll still need me, no matter whose flag flies over Gilead in the future.''

''What flaming Indians?'' his young wife demanded from the doorway, adding; ''They've all run away. You could never get the perishing barefoot beggars to sit through a sermon even when they were *here!*''

Then she vanished again, and from the sound of a door slamming somewhere in the house, she may have really meant it this time.

Perkins sighed and said, ''She's a bit high-strung. Indians seem to make her tense, and since those rather uncouth Nicaraguan soldiers moved into town—''

''This side of the river's already been occupied by Nicaraguan forces?'' Captain Gringo cut in as, before Perkins could answer, Gaston chimed in with, ''Which side, Grenada or Leon?''

Perkins looked puzzled and said, ''Heavens, how should I know? All I know is that a few nights ago, some chaps waving guns and machetes about dropped by. Didn't do anything much. Just yelled at me in Spanish a bit and posted some sort of public notice on the front of the church next door before they left. They behaved all right. Don't see why Olivia locked herself away like that. I have no idea whether they were supposed to be from . . . Grenada or Leon, you say?''

''We'd better have a look,'' said Captain Gringo, rising from the table. Perkins as well as Gaston followed him out the back door and around to the front of the church they hadn't noticed much about, so far. As they waded through the weeds, Gaston explained to the old minister, ''The jolly thugs of Grenada call themselves the Conservative Party while the gunslicks of Leon prefer to be called the Liberal Party. Please do not ask me why. The so-called Conservatives are inclined to be très radical, and the Liberals shoot anyone who asks to vote. One imagines even Jack the Ripper, whoever he may be, has *some* ideals he uses to justify his otherwise pointless viciousness. The last we heard, the Liberals were winning over to the west. But that was weeks ago, hein? The political situation in Nicaragua has never been too predictable from day to day.''

Perkins gulped and said, ''I say, which of these, ah, sides do you think would be most sympathetic to my Indians and my mission?''

''Neither,'' said Gaston flatly, glad to be on firmer ground. He explained, ''Pagan Indians afford target practice, no more, to your average Nicaraguan who wears pants at least on Sunday.''

''Oh, but my converts are Christians, too!''

''*Protestant* Christians, M'sieu?''

''Of course. We're Congregationalists.''

''I would not mention that to any Nicaraguan soldado of the unshaven type, M'sieu. They only recognize one form of Christianity, très vaguely, and neither you nor your Indian converts are it!''

By this time they'd all made it around to the front of the church, and Captain Gringo was already reading the military proclamation nailed to the wall. It was a cheaply printed broadside on the paper the color and texture of stale oatmeal. Perkins asked him what it said, explaining neither he nor his young wife knew enough Spanish to matter. Captain Gringo said, "I didn't think you could. The good news is that this property, including any good-looking women or other livestock on it, is reserved for the sole use of the general and his staff. The bad news is that this former British colony has been liberated in the name of the Nicaraguan people by one El Chino. It doesn't give the rank he claims. I guess his own guys know, and he doesn't care what *other* people think he is."

"What do *you* think he is?" asked Perkins, adding; "El Chino seems a rather rum name for a military governor, don't you think?"

"It would be, if that was what he was, Sir. 'Chino' can mean either a Chinaman, literally, or a type of moon-faced mestizo Hispanics nickname that way, as we use 'Slats,' or 'Pud.' In fairness to both sides in the ongoing civil war to the west, both the Liberals and Conservatives field more regular-type armies. Any military leader anyone in Nicaragua would be likely to recognize as even a semi-civilized enemy would call himself a colonel, a general or whatever. This El Chino character glories in a campesino nickname. He adds up to a guerrilla leader at best or, more likely, a plain old-fashioned bandito! How long did you say they posted this notice?"

"I told you, two, mayhaps three nights ago. Is it important?"

"It sure is, Rev. We've got to get you and more important, your woman the hell *out* of here! You say there are still some English on the south side of the river?"

"Yes, but we can't abandon everything we have, here!"

"What do you think you *have* here, damn it? With a whole town to loot, they just haven't gotten around to this part of Gilead yet. But according to El Chino, it's all his, in the name of the Nicaraguan people who may not know it's even here! The guy's cool. Whoever wrote that notice was literate. I think I see now who that steamer just delivered a load of something to, and I doubt like hell it was canned goods! Let's go; we'll talk about it on the way to Zion!"

"But we don't want to go to Zion!" Perkins protested, digging in his heels as Gaston tried to keep him moving through the weeds.

Captain Gringo said, "Let him go, Gaston. It's too far to drag a jackass, and his wife may have more sense!"

She did. She went right upstairs to start packing, even though her husband told her not to be silly. As soon as he was alone in the kitchen again with Captain Gringo and Gaston, the minister said, "I say, now you've gone too far! A wife's place is with her husband, and I see no reason to desert my mission. So we're not going anywhere, and that's final!"

Captain Gringo shrugged and said, "You've no idea how final it can get once a guerrilla leader consolidates his position and turns his boys loose for fun and games! This siesta time will be over in less than three hours. So let's talk about how far we can get between now and then. You know this layout better than we do, Rev. The parts of town we've seen so far look like a little bit of England out to lunch. Which way's the native quarter where less Anglo-Saxon types might feel more at home?"

Perkins shrugged and pointed at the blank kitchen wall to the north as he said, "The unofficial but strictly enforced deadline is two streets over. I wanted to build my mission in the Mosquito barrio or at least closer. But the people who sent me had already bought this older church the Anglicans built back in the fifties, so—"

"Never mind how any of us got *here*," Captain Gringo cut in. "I'm talking about getting us to *there!* There would be the parts of the colony still under British control so that would be Zion, south of the river, right? How do we get across? I didn't notice any bridges as we approached the shore awhile back."

Perkins prissed his lips and said, "There's a shallow ford, if you know where to cross. It's too deep east and west of the ford."

Captain Gringo nodded firmly and said, "Bueno. That's another reason you're coming with us. You know the way. We don't. You'd better just pack enough to carry. No more than a change of clothes, a few keepsakes you just have to have and, of course, any money you have on hand."

"I don't have enough money for even bandits to worry about, and I'm not coming with you, either. Neither is my wife. I don't understand these dramatics at all. This General Chino has been here in Gilead at least seventy-two hours, and as you see, he hasn't made a move against us since they posted that sign putting us under his personal protection!"

Captain Gringo snorted in disgust and said, "A chicken is under the personal protection of its owner, too, until the owner gets around to *plucking* it! I'm not sure why anyone would want to pluck you personally, Rev. But your wife's a lot prettier, and I'm using *pluck* as the intended verb because we're close to a church."

He moved to the window, glanced out to see nothing moving out there in the midday heat, then shot an anxious look at the doorway Olivia had left by as he muttered, "Thank God I didn't tell her to change her dress. How long do you think we can give her, Gaston?"

Gaston leaned against the cold kitchen stove, lighting another smoke with a thoughtful frown before he replied, "Nothing très dramatique should occur before three or later, Dick. But have you thought this matter all the way through? My sainted Aunt Fifi, the one who was attractive enough to pick pockets *inside* the Paris Opera, once told me, as we were making love, never to jump into the fire from the frying pan unless the frying pan was unusually hot, hein?"

"You stupid bastard, the heat out there's the only thing that's keeping a lid on the usual guerrilla routine!"

Gaston shook his head and said, "Mais non, this Protestant man of the cloth, while of course in serious error about the hereafter, makes an interesting point or more, Dick. This unwashed species of Chino does seem to be an unusually cool leader, and since one doubts even a quarter of his men can *read*, they must have been *told* to leave these people alone and, miracle of miracles, they must be under unusually good control, for guerrillas.''

''Maybe. But the British constabulary still holding out south of the river have to be even less likely to start looting and raping in the near future, like as soon as it's cool enough!''

''Oui, but on the other hand, wouldn't British constabularies be more inclined to arrest us than outlaws who, for all we know, may welcome an extra pair of skilled fighters with open arms?''

Captain Gringo shot a warning glance at the minister seated stubbornly at the table and told Gaston, ''You've got a mighty open *mouth*, too! But okay, let's try that on for size and see how it fits. It feels too snug for *me*, old chum! In the first place, this Chino probably thinks he's a chief. So he'd want lots of little Indians, not officers, under him. In the second place, we're soldiers of fortune, not bandits!''

Gaston shrugged and said, ''Merde alors, there you go acting picky again. The only difference between a bandit and a soldier is the size of his gang. Robert E. Lee and the late Jessee James shared much the same views on fighting the U.S. Federal Government. The only difference was the number of followers each had, non?''

Captain Gringo grinned despite himself, but said, ''Let's not get into semantics. Let's just get the hell out of here. The British authorities across the creek have no way of knowing we're on their shit list, if only you don't tell them. The people on this side of the creek have already told us this El Chino is worse company that the Brits.''

''They have? Mais how? Save for these innocents here, we have not even met a native of this Gilead, let alone been told to avoid El Chino, Dick.''

''You have to see it in writing, you jerk-off? El Chino is one of their own, yet the natives as well as the English settlers, here, have all run away from him! How come, if he's such a swell guy? You know how these operations usually go, Gaston. God knows you've taken part in enough so-called liberations.''

Gaston sighed and said, ''Oui, the usual form calls for

dancing in the streets, shouts of Viva Whoever and a general looting of the few in town who just can't avoid being tagged as the former oppression. The impoverished campesino types, as you say, usually welcome invading armies as probably no worse and possibly better than the bullies they know better and, hmm, come to think of it, most Latins find the English très fatigue. So to run to the flag of Victoria for protection from one of their own . . ."

"That's what I just said. So where the hell is that dame?"

As if she'd been waiting offstage for her entrance cue, Olivia came in carrying a carpet bag too heavy for her, and they noticed she'd pinned on a little straw hat with fake cherries on it as well. Her husband looked up and said, "Dear Heart, you look silly in that outfit, and I forbid you to leave with these gentlemen. For one thing, there's no reason for you to run away; and for another I fear these gentlemen are not exactly gentlemen!"

Captain Gringo looked at Gaston and growled, "You and your big mouth. Come on, Rev. We can argue about it along the way."

Perkins shook his head stubbornly and braced himself in his chair as if daring them to pick him up, chair and all, and carry him. But that would have been silly even had it been twenty degrees cooler. So Captain Gringo nodded grimly and said, "Right. I'll take the lead Gaston. You'd better help the lady with that bag."

He stepped out the back door without looking back to see if Gaston was doing as he was told. He was more worried about guys he didn't know as well. But not even a fly was stirring outside in the afternoon steam bath. So he started down the steps and heard both the boot heels of Gaston and the high-button shoes of Olivia following— even though old Hiram Perkins was bleating like a sheep after them.

Captain Gringo wanted to get out of the open, poco tiempo, so he legged it off the church grounds, across a deserted street, into the first alley running south he could get them into. It was shadier albeit no cooler in the alley. Off in the distance, Perkins was still bleating something about his wife not coming back if she persisted in avoiding gang rape. Captain Gringo stopped to get his bearings, turned to Olivia and said, "Look, there's an outside chance he's right, and I wouldn't want to break up a happy marriage."

She shrugged and said, "Neither would I. Why are we just standing here?"

He said, "It's always a good idea to know where you're going before you go there. Do you know the way to the ford across the Mission River?"

She said, "Of course. Once I'm near it, I mean. What are we doing in this perishing alley?"

"Trying not to perish. If El Chino has any patrols out at all, they'll be patrolling the main streets, I hope. I know how to get us to the river. How are you doing with that bag, Gaston?"

Gaston groaned, "Badly. I might have known an Englishwoman would insist on bringing along her tea service. We French have more experience with sudden emergencies. It is more practique to keep the family fortune small and portable in the form of a few gold coins in a teapot one can leave *behind!*"

Captain Gringo could see the wiry little Frenchman wasn't really having trouble with the girl's things, and, what the hell, it was all she had. So he just said, "All right, let's keep going, and keep it down to a roar. The houses on either side *look* deserted, but you just never know."

They made it down to the end of the block, scooted across the dirt street and down another, and so forth until Olivia said the river was somewhere just ahead. Captain Gringo had already figured as much, given the modest size of the settlement. He told Gaston and the girl to sit tight while he scouted the ford, adding, "If they have a road-block set up anywhere, that will be it. Maybe you'd better duck into that house, there. It looks empty, and you won't want to be caught in the open if I run into trouble."

But Gaston had already opened the back gate and was leading the girl through the backyard weeds toward the kitchen door of the mustard frame bungalow. So Captain

Gringo moved on without further elaboration. Gaston would know what to do if he heard pistol shots or worse. The old pro could talk the horns off a billy goat when there was nothing important to talk about. But the nice thing about working with a partner who'd been in the game far longer than you had was that he tended to read your mind when the chips were down.

Captain Gringo moved to the end of the alley, and, sure enough, there was a wall of gumbo-limbo and sea grape instead of another block across the muddy street. Through the few gaps in the wild running spinach, he could see the gleam of sunlight on water. He eased out of the alley to follow the wider street west, since he could see it dead-ended to the east no more than two blocks away. He saw water-filled cartwheel ruts in the red clay ahead. They figured, if he was heading for the ford. The last east-west wagon trace north of the river lay close enough to sea level to stay muddy all the time. The unusually deep ruts indicated recent heavy moving, and they'd naturally move their furniture across the river the only place one could.

As he eased closer, he spotted movement down the road ahead and crabbed sideways behind a clump of sea grape, drawing his .38. Then he cursed, but very quietly, as he saw what was going on up that way. A guy wearing a white cotton campesino outfit, a big straw sombrero and more ammunition bandoleers than anyone but a poor shot could possibly ever need was taking a leak against a pepper tree. From the way sunlight was bouncing off his big hat, there had to be a break in the riverside vegetation just south of him. So this single pisser was standing guard at the only ford across the pissy river!

One-on-one wasn't enough to stop Captain Gringo, but the first thing he had to find out was whether the pisser was *alone* up that way. He waited until the bandito finished watering the tree and turned away. Then he dashed back across the street into another alley and vaulted a backyard fence to crouch low in the weeds and work his way a bit farther west.

It didn't work. He got as far as the rear of the house, peered out through the pickets of its side-fencing and saw

he didn't have a decent view into the gap of the crossing
from this angle. He could see his pisser, or someone,
moving about in a tunnel-archway of riverside trees and
underbrush. But he had to get closer for a clear view.

That was what houses with back doors were made for.
He moved to the back door, tried the latch and found it
was locked. He called the locked door a dreadful thing.
The door looked too solid to kick in without bringing the
one-or-more guards less than fifty yards away on the
double. So he holstered his .38, took out his pocketknife
and slid a blade between the lock and jamb to see if by any
chance it was a spring-latch job.

It was. He grinned as the door popped open with a little
chirp no louder than a cricket. Then, since people might
wonder what even a cricket was doing up and about during
La Siesta, he ducked inside and closed the door silently
after him.

The house, like the others he and Gaston had explored
earlier, was deserted, or at least it seemed to be until he
heard someone whispering—somewhere *inside* the dank
and dark interior with him!

He got the gun out again, fast, and eased toward the
front of the house on the balls of his feet. The whispering
was coming from the front parlor. As he moved closer, he
could make out a few words. It sounded like a woman,
whispering in Spanish, scared as hell.

The pretty little mestiza and her older but not-bad
female companion crouched near a window in the front
room looked even more frightened as Captain Gringo
popped in on them, .38 muzzle trained, to snap, "Congeles!
One sound, one move, and you're both dead!"

The older one disobeyed him. She made the sign of the
cross. But Captain Gringo figured that was fair, so he
didn't shoot her. He moved in closer, lowering the muzzle
of his .38 as he saw they were alone, unarmed and
obviously scared skinny. He said, "Bueno. What's going
on here?"

The older woman sobbed. "Please don't do it to my
daughter! Take me, if you must have a woman. But have

mercy on my Rosalita. She is still a virgin. She would not know for how to give you a good time anyway, see?''

The younger girl said, "Oh, Mother," as Captain Gringo smiled down at them both and said, "Let's all calm down. We may be on the same side, even if this used to be an English address. Why are the two of you hiding here?''

The girl called Rosalita, who seemed able to size men up more quickly than her mother, considering, said, "We have been trying for to get south, behind the British lines. But El Chino has hombres, muy malo hombres, blocking the only way across to safety!''

He put his gun back under his jacket as he moved to join them at the window. He stayed upright but out of line of the dusty glass as he risked a peek around the edge and grunted, "When you're right, you're right, damn it!''

From this vantage, he could see into the green archway. He didn't like what he saw at all. There was more than one pisser on guard. There were *four* of the pissers. Two of them lounged behind the breech of a Maxim machine gun aimed the other way, across the muddy, sluggish shallows of the ford. He couldn't see, from here, what the Brits on the other shore were doing about all this, if anything. He told the two mestizas, "I think they're there to make sure nobody crosses from the south. But that's still not doing *us* much good.''

Rosalita asked brightly, "Could you shoot them for us so we could go south to join the Anglo family we used to work for? You have a gun, and you look muy macho, Senor . . . ?''

"I am called Dick," he replied, "and taking on four guys armed with four carbines and a machine gun wouldn't be macho, it would be just plain dumb. There has to be a better way. I've got to sneak back and pick up my own friends. Do you muchachas really want to get to Zion that much? Don't you have anyone on your side left on this side of the river?''

The older woman said simply, "Who can say who one's friends are at times like these, Senor Deek? My daughter, as you see, is most beautiful; men are men, whether they marched in with those guerrillas or have simply admired her in the past, eh? There are no policia left in Gilead. The only police left are across the river in Zion. Los Anglos do not rape virgins. We do not intend to find out, the hard way, how our so-called liberator, El Chino, feels about such matters.''

He shrugged and said, ''I'm not sure I trust a Nicaraguan liberator who calls himself a Chinaman, either. Bueno. If you two want to tag along, let's go. This place can't be as safe as the place my other friends hang out in these days.''

He started for the back door. Behind him, he heard the mother whisper, ''Pero no! How do we know we can trust him?'' But her daughter whispered back, ''Oh Mother, he has a gun and I'm *still* a virgin, damn it. Let's chance it. We can't stay here!''

So Captain Gringo wasn't surprised when they followed him out the back way, chattering like magpies until he warned them to keep it down, adding, ''Let's not tell them where we are or where we're going. Let's make them guess.''

Knowing now what the setup was and where he was going, it took Captain Gringo only a few minutes to lead the two native women to the house where Gaston and Olivia were holed up. As he introduced everyone, Gaston kissed the older mestiza's hand, told her he was enchanted and added in English to Captain Gringo, ''Eh bien, it's about time you showed some consideration of your elders.''

The older woman, whose name turned out to be Filipa, made the sign of the cross again and told her daughter, ''Now I *know* we're going to be raped, you stubborn child!'' So Captain Gringo knew they'd picked up some English while working for British employers, and there went any chance to tell Gaston to for Chrissake calm down a bit. He filled the Frenchman in on the outpost at the ford, and Gaston said, ''It sounds like a Mexican standoff, then. The British constabulary, having circled the wagons while they wait for their government to evacuate them, no doubt have the far side of our adorable crossing zeroed in as well. But they've given up on this side of the river.''

''How do you know?''

''Merde alors, do you really think a band of guerrillas

moving in to take advantage of the confusion could stand up to an all-out attack by a determined British constabulary, Dick?''

Captain Gringo shrugged and said, ''Depends on how many there might be on either side. The Brits learned in the Zulu Wars that trained soldiers can only stand off so many determined screamers at a time, and the constabulary aren't real soldiers. They're just colonial police trained to handle street fighters in sensible numbers. I've no idea of the numbers involved, here and now, but El Chino has at least one no-kidding machine gun.''

Gaston wrinkled his nose and said, ''Oui, so now we have a better idea what was in those crates our adorable skipper unloaded for El Chino earlier today. I wonder how on earth the guerrilla *paid* for them.''

It was a good question. Captain Gringo didn't have the answer. So her turned to Olivia Perkins to ask her, ''Could your friends and neighbors have neglected to move a bank or two across the river in the sudden rush?''

She shook her head and replied, ''Coo, not bloody likely. Hardly anyone took the evacuation seriously until the colonial blokes moved the branch bank and post office down to Zion!''

He frowned and said, ''Hmm, I take it, then, that Zion is the bigger, more important half of the colony?''

She said, ''Zion's more than half. It's where the government house and most of the business firms are, or were. It's hard to say what we'll find there, now that Her Bloody Majesty's giving it all back to the niggers like a chump!''

He shot her a warning glance and said, ''I think they'd rather be called Nicaraguans. Hardly anyone around here has obvious African blood, Doll.''

''If you say so.'' She shrugged, adding, ''I was brought up to call anyone who wasn't white a nigger.''

He didn't doubt that, and it was probably a little late to suggest better race relations to a lady who thought God was an Englishman. He turned back to Gaston and said, ''You may be right. It doesn't make much sense, but it could be the usual standoff. The question before the house is, How do we get over to the side that sounds more civilized?''

Gaston said, "By broad daylight, two thirty-eights against four carbines and a machine gun?"

"The machine gun's mounted on a tripod, facing the other way."

"Merde alors, a British machine gun is no doubt facing this way from the other side, as well! I know good soldiers are trained to consider what they may be shooting at before they open fire, my eternal optimist, but I would not wish to risk my poor old derriere on the goodwill of a no-doubt très tense British machine-gun crew as I charged out of the smoke of a gunfight at them. So I do not intend to!"

Captain Gringo nodded soberly and said, "It would be safer to swim, at that." Then he turned to the three women to ask if any of them felt up to a moonlight swim across the Mission River.

Olivia Perkins said she didn't know how to swim. Rosalita said she could swim a little. But her mother said, "No you can't. Not across *that* river, in the *dark*! Have you forgotten the time the shark took Pedro Holquin, in the shallows as he spear-fished by moonlight?"

This time it was Rosalita's turn to make the sign of the cross. Captain Gringo shrugged and said, "I didn't want to get my hair wet so soon after setting it anyway. Gaston, has it occurred to you all these deserted houses are made of wood, and that wood *floats*?"

"Too noisy," Gaston objected, adding: "It would of course be soup of the duck to improvise a raft of house timbers. But would you not wonder, if you were on guard in a part of town you were told was deserted, why you heard hammering in the neighborhood?"

"Okay, so we move to another neighborhood. The riverside street runs a couple of blocks seaward. They won't have it guarded down that way, because it's a dead end. If we sort of tear apart the last house down that way, working in the backyard, tapping like brownies with our gun butts or, hell, maybe we can find some *rope*—"

Then he and everyone else in the house froze, because a not too friendly voice was calling from outside the house, "Hey, Captain Gringo, are you in there? Sure, we know you're in there!"

The words were in Spanish. The intent was less clear. So Captain Gringo put a finger to his lips for silence as he moved to the nearest rear window, softly hissing, "Gaston?" And Gaston headed for the front windows to check that angle out without having any pictures drawn on the blackboard for him.

There were at least a half dozen guys, dressed buscadero flashy, leaning over the rear fence of the house. A couple had their carbine barrels poking Captains Gringo's way through the tops of the pickets, but not aimed at anything in particular. The guy doing the talking had painted his straw sombrero park-bench green with shiny deck enamel and wore a brighter green shirt under his crossed bandoleers. So Captain Gringo wasn't too suprised to hear him shout, "I am called El Repollo, I am segundo to El Chino and I only wish for to be your amigo, see?"

Captain Gringo didn't answer. He wasn't sure he wanted to make friends with a guy who said he was a cabbage working for a Chinaman.

Rosalita moved close enough to nudge the tall American's elbow as she murmured, "Your friend the Frenchman says to tell you they are out front, as well. He says he has the front door covered, but that he wishes you would hurry up and think of something most clever, Deek!"

He couldn't. He cracked the window open. Flying glass in the face was always annoying, anyway, and the bastards knew they had the address right, so what the hell. He called out, "Who is this Captain Gringo you speak of, my little cabbage?"

"Hey, that is no way for to talk. I am one *big* cabbage, so that is why they call me *El* Repollo, not *Uno* Repollo, see?"

"I stand corrected. Who's this Captain Gringo supposed to be?"

"Don't be modest, Captain Gringo. Everybody know who you are. You and your amigo, Gaston Verrier from the Mexican Army of Juarez, fought the lousy bastard Nicaraguan Liberal Party not long ago. That makes us comrades in arms, since we have fought the same lousy bastards many times, see?"

"Are you guys with the Grenada side?"

"Hey, bite your tongue, the Conservatives are lousy bastards, too. Besides, we know you have fought *them* too! Like ourselves, you fight bastards where you find them, eh?"

"Well, it does seem a little hard to avoid running into bastards in Nicaragua these days."

El Repollo didn't get it. He called back, "Es verdad, Amigo. Those stuck-up sissies with their blue Spanish blood and book-learning use the rest of us for target practice no matter what party they say they belong to. But, look, for why are we shouting back and forth like fishwives, eh? Come on out. El Chino has been wishing for to have a word with you ever since he heard you were in town."

"Really? Who told him we'd arrived?"

"A little bird, of course. How many blond giants jump a ship with a little gray cat of a Frenchman on any given day, eh?"

By this time Gaston had joined him at the window, saying, "Ten or more out front, and what was that about my looking feline?"

"That mate who spotted us must have mentioned us to the guys they were running guns to, damn it. They've put two and two together pretty good. What do you think we ought to do about it?"

Outside, El Repollo was insisting, "Hey, no shit, it's *hot* out here, hombres!"

So Gaston shrugged and said, "They know they have us outgunned in a frame structure never meant for stopping bullets."

Captain Gringo glanced back at the three nervous-looking women who seemed to be depending on him and muttered, "Yeah, one good fusillade would make one hell of a mess on the linoleum. It's time to salvage what we can, I guess. See if you can find a place for them to hide while I stall."

Outside, the guerrilla leader fired his pistol, fortunately straight up, and yelled, "What's the matter with you, Yanqui? This is no time for to act coy with us! El Chino told me his wished for to see you, and I have to take you to him one way or the other, eh?''

Captain Gringo called out, "We have to consider your terms, first. So let's hear them.''

El Repollo looked confused, then bellowed, "Terms, what the fuck are you talking about? Did I say anything about terms? Did I ask for you to surrender? I only said El Chino wants to talk to you, and by the balls of Christ, that is where I mean to take you!''

Gaston rejoined Captain Gringo at the window, saying, "Crawl space under the low pitched roof. Hotter than a whore's pillow up there, of course, but there is no cellar, so—''

"Good thinking. Most of these guys never heard of an attic," Captain Gringo cut in, adding: "Did they pull the ladder up after them?''

Gaston shook his head and said, "There was no ladder. Simply a trapdoor in a hall closet one sincerely hopes no less cultivated criminal will notice. The native women know what to do as soon as it's dark. I have their address in the native quarter and—''

"*Now* who's being an optimist?'' Captain Gringo cut in, opening the door to call out, "Don't get your shit hot. We're coming out.'' Then he murmured to Gaston in a softer tone, "They may be on the level. We'll know in a minute. I don't intend to give my gun up without a fight. Do you?''

"Do I look like a man who enjoys death by slow torture? Lead on, my Mac of Duff. If we go down fighting in the next few minutes, you must forgive me for not having had time to leave you in my will, hein?''

To call El Repollo pleasant would have been stretching it, but he didn't even mention their guns, and nobody pointed guns directly at the two soldiers of fortune as they headed back across town with their newfound friends, if that too wasn't stretching it some.

As they passed by the church and entered the native barrio of Gilead, it began to look, in fact, as if everyone had been overreacting a bit. There weren't too many people out on the dirt streets laid out more crookedly between less imposing housing, but it was, after all, still siesta time and there were a few pigs and chickens in evidence, still alive and well, so El Chino's boys were acting well-behaved indeed for Central American guerrillas.

The big man himself was holding court in a frame schoolhouse the colonial authorities had once painted battleship gray instead of red. El Chino was seated behind a desk in the principal's office, and the first thing they noticed about him was that he wasn't big at all. He was even smaller than Gaston, and didn't fit his nickname, either. El Chino had neither the moon face nor chunky build of the Indian type that Hispanics seemed to find oriental in appearance. He was a little dried-up guy with sharp features that hinted at a little pure Spanish, a little Aztec, or even Apache, and a lot of cold cunning. He wore ammo bandoleers across his military shirt, of course. Guys who led guerrilla armies were supposed to look like guerillas. His big black sombrero, at the moment was atop the head of the Junoesque lady perched with one cheek of her shapely ass on one corner of the desk. She had lots of ammunition across her chest, too. So despite the fact she wore no blouse above her flouncy red fandango skirts, one couldn't see both her nipples at once. She looked less friendly than the little skinny guy who owned her. El Chino smiled up at the soldiers of fortune and told them it was so good of them to drop by. Then he spoiled it all by looking beyond them at El Repollo lounging in the doorway, to ask, "Where is the redheaded Protestant puta?"

El Repollo said, "Before God, I do not know, Jefe. She was not with these two when we caught up with them near the river."

El Chino stared thoughtfully at Captain Gringo, as if he expected his reluctant visitor to say something. Captain Gringo asked, "Are we talking about La Señora Perkins, from the Congregational Church?"

"We are. I just assured her husband we did not have her. So tell me, Captain Gringo, who has her?"

The American shrugged and said, "Don't look at us. Ain't nobody here but us chickens."

"You left the church with her, no?"

"We sure did. She was carrying a lot of stuff and moved slow as a sick snail. Next thing we knew, your boys caught up with us; and when we looked around for the dame, she just wasn't there. Maybe she ran off when she saw all those guys with guns, eh?"

El Chino raised an eyebrow at El Repollo, who said, "There was nobody in the house with them, Jefe. I had one of my men look inside before we left. They could be telling the truth. It happens, and you know how some women are when they meet strangers."

El Chino said, "Send some muchachos back for to comb the whole neighborhood, then. I told its old owner there was no need for to worry about his pig, and I do not wish for to be called a liar, even by a Protestant. Tell the ones you send that if they bring her back raped, or even frightened, I shall shoot them in front of their own people and then shoot their people. This is no time for to make needless enemies, and the old Englishman may still be useful to us."

El Repollo said he'd get right on it. As he left, his place in the doorway was taken by another guy with a gun, repeat gun, no matter how politely he wore it at the moment.

El Chino smiled up at his guests again and said, "Bueno. As you see, I am a sensible person as well as a great leader. I know what you may have heard about me. My enemies are always saying bad things about me. But it is not true about those nuns, and I was not the one who burned down the pueblo of San Mateo. I was only there for to rob the bank. The fire started by accident as we were riding out. I am gentle as a lamb, to people who know better than to cross me."

Captain Gringo smiled thinly and replied, "Remind me never to cross you, then, El Chino."

"I just did. I suppose you are wondering for why I had you brought here?"

"Well, I'm sort of relieved to suspect it wasn't to steal our boots."

"I prefer my boots custom-made. I like to have money for other luxuries as well. So you see, we are both after the same thing."

"We are?" Captain Gringo frowned, still in the dark.

El Chino chuckled and said, "They told me you played poker as well as lone-wolf. Bueno, I admire a man who is serious about money. We never had enough when I was growing up." He reached out to place a casual hand in his desk decoration's skirted lap as he added, "With money, and the power money brings with it, one can have anything one wants. Ask Estralita, here."

The big buxom brunette said, "Es verdad," and pulled up her skirt to put El Chino's skinny brown hand between her naked thighs. He fondled her fuzz absently as he told Captain Gringo, "Enough of this fencing with words. Are you two in with me or not?"

Captain Gringo tried to keep his eyes out of Estralita's exposed lap as he said, "We might be if we knew what you were talking about. I don't think it could be your adelita. But I don't see anything else around here I'd want in on."

El Chino laughed, or at least sort of cackled, and said, "You can have some of this too, if that is your price."

The brunette looked startled and pouted. "Oh Jefe, what kind of a muchacha do you think I am?"

The old man removed his hand from her snatch and wiped it on her skirt as he replied, "Any kind of a muchacha I wish for you to be, of course. If I require you to fuck my dog, you will fuck my dog, no?"

"But, Jefe, you do not have a dog!"

"That is unimportant. If I want for you to fuck a dog, I shall send for one and you will fuck it. Meanwhile, get out of here for now. We have business for to discuss, and men can't talk sense with hard-ons."

The big brunette sighed, got off the desk and replaced

her butt with the big black sombrero before sulking out, muttering something about not listening to her momma.

El Chino told the guard in the doorway to get lost, too. The younger and much bigger guerrilla objected, "But, Jefe, there are two of them, and El Repollo may have failed for to mention they still have their guns on under those jackets!"

The old man snorted in disgust and said, "Leave us, damn the milk of your mother! Do I look like a man who does not know how to look out for himself?"

The guard shrugged, stepped out, and closed the door behind the soldiers of fortune. El Chino said, "Bueno. Don't get ideas. I have a forty-five in my lap and my men are all around out there."

Captain Gringo laughed easily and said, "El Repollo told us this would be a friendly visit. We had our chance to shoot it out with you guys long before we got here."

El Chino said, "No, you didn't. When I heard you were after the money, too, I sent enough men for to handle even *you*, Captain Gringo!"

"We were wondering about that. Could we cut all this bullshit and get to the point?"

Gaston added, "Oui, despite all the dramatiques, we have no idea what you are talking about. But since you just mentioned *money*, I assure you that you have our undivided attention!"

El Chino looked disgusted and said, "We still have to mince words? Very well, to show you how useless it is to attempt it on your own, I shall begin at the beginning. I know who you are. You are Ricardo Walker, also and better known as Captain Gringo; and you my innocent French friend, are the notorious Gaston Verrier. You are both wanted in more places, for more crimes, then even I am! Do you deny this?"

Gaston said, "You would know your own history better than we would. Mais this unruly child and I have made *some* noise in our travels that seems to have upset some people."

El Chino said, "So now we find you here, in the crown colony of Mission Bay, as the British are in the process of evacuating it. I suppose you are going to tell me, next, you just jumped ship to get tattooed? You are both wanted by the British government. You never would have risked your heads in a British colony unless you had a damned good reason!''

"That's true," said Captain Gringo—honestly enough, when one thought about it.

So El Chino leaned back and said, "Now we are getting someplace. Like us, you somehow learned of the gold bullion and specie the colonial authorities kept here on hand and will *keep* here on hand until they complete their evacuation, no?''

Captain Gringo knew the old rogue would never believe him if he said the idea had never occurred to him before. So he nodded and said, "Right. We heard aboard the ship about the Brits giving this colony back to the Indians. So, yeah, we sneaked ashore to see if there was any chance to pick up loose change in the confusion. But the damned boat left without us; and between you and me, we don't know where the hell they have the colonial funds right now.''

El Chino said, "I do. Across the river in the vaults of the government house. It was there all the time. We hoped to find at least *some* money in the bank here in Gilead. But they'd cleaned it out before we arrived. Someone must have told them we were coming for to take official possession for Nicaragua, and if I find out who—''

"Don't look at us," Captain Gringo cut in as Gaston added: "Oui, we only arrived a few short hours ago. Besides, even a Protestant banker may have guessed some, ah, patriots might show up before the official transfer of the property to its former owners, hein?''

El Chino brushed at his face if Gaston's words were flies and said, "It is not important. The money is all on the wrong side of the river. The overly tidy English left nothing worth looting on this side. Once they have transportation arranged for the Zion settlement, they mean to leave nothing for us on the *other* side of the river, either—and I ask you, is this just payment for the years they held this Nicaraguan land unlawfully?''

Gaston soothed, "Mais non, they have always had a reputation as poor tippers. May one ask how long the très sneaky English intend to hold out, south of the river?"

El Chino said, "They plan for to evacuate in stages, women and children first for some strange reason. Do I look like a man who does not like women and children? They know we are here, of course. My scouts tell me they've mounted their own outposts just across the river. But getting back to more important matters, I have been assured the colonial funds, along with the flag, records and so forth, will be leaving last. The British have only so many merchant vessels charted for to take out their colonists and their belongings. Some few have already left. Most are still there. We have to take Zion before the next convoy arrives."

It would have been stupid to ask a self-glorified bandit why he wanted to occupy a town before they even had a chance to remove the furniture. So Captain Gringo asked, "Wouldn't it be smarter to *let* them evacuate most of the non combatants, Jefe?"

El Chino looked pleased to be called "Chief," but not at all pleased with the suggestion. He asked, "Would *you* like to attack British constabulary who have a clear field of fire and only their own hides to worry about? They told me you two were professional soldiers, damn it!"

Captain Gringo growled, "We are. That's why women and kids in the way seem, well, for one thing, in the way. Firefights can get complicated enough when you know who to aim at on the other side."

El Chino said, "I fail to see what is so complicated about it. One aims at everybody on the other side, of course! They tell me you are an ace machine-gunner, Captain Gringo, and that you, Gaston, are an old artilleryman who can drop a shell in a barrel from five kilometers away. Es verdad?"

Gaston shrugged modestly and said, "I only promise results at three kilometers, and I prefer no children in the barrel at the time."

El Chino said, "If they do not wish for to see noncombatants hurt, they had better avoid combat with me, then! I have four new Maxims, and my men have carbines that fire the same ammunition. How does that sound to you, Caballeros?"

Captain Gringo said, "Not so hot. The Brits are sure to have at least some automatic weapons—and guys who've been trained to use them better than your guys, no offense."

El Chino nodded soberly and said, "That is for why I was so pleased to hear the two of you were in town. There is only a handful of Royal Marines to the south, posted for to guard the Royal Governor. Most of their forces will be mere policia, more accustomed to fighting with nightsticks than rifles, see?"

"What about old vets?"

"Vets? What vets? Nobody told me anything about vets, and what is a vet in the first place?"

"Ex-army, -navy, or worse yet, -Royal Marines," said Captain Gringo, explaining further: "When guys get out of the British military services, they tend to go out to the colonies a lot; and if there's one thing British colonial policy has produced in this century, it's old vets of more wars than you could shake a stick at. Old Queen Vickie's had her proper cockneys swapping rounds with everyone from Afghans to Zulu since before even you were born, Jefe, and some cockneys grow up sort of tough to begin with. You have to figure on at least half the able-bodied civilians on the other side to be pretty good in a scrap."

"Bah, half of them are women and children!"

"That's what I just said. Don't bank on every female lime-juicer to throw nothing but tea crumpets at you, either. Lots of girls from the horsey set shoot grouse when the fox is out of season."

Gaston said, "We still have not discussed *artillery*, my bloodthirsty children. There is always at least one field gun in every British port of call. They have this odd habit of shooting at the sunset with it when not saluting ships and all that rot the English seem to enjoy. Did I hear mention of artillery on this side of the river, just now?"

El Chino shifted in his seat uncomfortably and said, "It is on the way. I just sent a heavy combat patrol for to capture an outpost of the Liberales, over to the west. It should be arriving any moment now."

"But you don't have even one big gun right now?" Captain Gringo insisted, groping for *some* damned way to get the old bandit to reconsider his options. He didn't owe the lime-juicers on the south side of the river anything, and they could probably fight off what amounted to untrained infantry in any case, but the idea of women and children anywhere near a serious firefight made him want to puke.

El Chino seemed more upset about losing his own unwashed and older boys. He scowled down at the desktop and said, "We will have artillery when it is time for to move. Meanwhile, now that you two have joined my army of liberation, we had better see about rations and quarters for you, no?"

Captain Gringo just wanted to get out of there before he lost his temper. But Gaston had to ask, "Eh bien, but what about *pay* in this man's species of army, Mon Generale?"

El Chino had no sense of humor. He scowled and answered, "Pay? Pay? You take me for a fool who pays money to men when they are not *fighting* for me? I arm my people. I feed my people. I share the loot they win for me with my people. Is not that pay enough for an hombre who does not squat down for to piss?"

Before either of them could tell El Chino what they thought of his all-too-common financial views, Estralita came back in to announce, "Your banquero just sent a runner to ask for why you are keeping him waiting, Jefe. You have an afternoon appointment with him, remember?"

El Chino scowled and snapped, "Of course I remember. Do I look absentminded? La Siesta will not end for at least another half hour. Who ever heard of keeping business appointments during La Siesta? The miser has no soul."

Estralita shrugged and started to leave; but El Chino told her, "Wait. These hombres are with us. So see that they have something for to eat, someplace for to sleep and somebody for to sleep with. Tell the others nobody but me is allowed to pick on them."

The buxom brunette nodded but asked, "What should I tell that runner?" And the old man answered, "Nada. By the time he could get back, La Siesta will be over in any case. Let El Banquero sweat a few momentos. It will be good for his character. What are you waiting for, damn it? Did I not just give you orders regarding these two hombres?''

Estralita told Captain Gringo and Gaston to follow her. So they did. She led them outside and took off across the schoolyard ahead of them, not looking back, as if she didn't give a damn either way.

They'd noticed the campesina girl's Spanish was uncultivated and had her figured as illiterate. So Gaston assumed her English had to be even lousier and muttered, ''I have admired short bullies, and I detest a man who lies just for practice. Put them together, and merde alors, one begins to pine for fresher air. The smell of fish around here is overwhelming, and I am not speaking of our unwashed guide. I am speaking of the fish of Denmark!''

Captain Gringo had noticed less than an hour before that some barefoot campesinas spoke English. So he told Gaston to knock it off and just go along with the gag, for now.

Estralita led them down a side street too narrow for easy traffic and too wide for decent shade. As she stopped and turned in front of a larger corrugated sheet-iron structure, a tiny whistle tooted in the middle distance and Captain Gringo muttered, ''What the hell?'' as he glanced up to see puffs of oily black smoke above the rooftops down the street.

Estralita said, ''You are not supposed to go down that way. It is a military secret that we have the railroad running again. Come inside. I shall issue you your rations now.''

They congratulated her on how well she kept military secrets and followed her into what seemed to be some sort of warehouse they doubted the guerrillas had built.

Bales, crates and gunnysacks were stacked all around in a slipshod way. Captain Gringo spotted some crates in a corner he'd last seen being unloaded from the SS *Trinidad*, but didn't comment on them. Estralita patted a pile of sacks as if it were a pony and said, ''Most of this is cornmeal and beans. There may be some coffee in the pile. Our general has commandeered all the supplies we could possibly use from the local pobrecitos. So help yourself to such food as you require. You can recruit your own women for to cook it for you, and when you wish for to bed down, just go into any house none of our other muchachos have taken over and make yourselves at home. There are plenty of empty houses in this barrio now. But if you see one you like and someone is still dwelling there, just tell them to get out and I am sure they will.''

Captain Gringo said he was sure they would, too. Then he asked her if they were free to choose local girls as adelitas; and Estralita replied, "Of course. Mess with a woman one of our soldados has already chosen and he will try for to kill you. But why fight over women when there are so many to go around, eh?''

"I get the picture. But I'll bet by now all the really good-looking women have been taken, eh? I mean no disrespect to your own soldado, but I have to admit he knows how to pick 'em.''

For the first time since they'd seen her, the big tough broad smiled. She even fluttered her lashes. But she said, "I must get back, before he suspects me of flirting with younger hombres.'' She moved to the doorway again, but turned in it to add with an injured expression, "It is not true I fuck dogs. I do not even have a cat. I used to have a cat, but El Chino shot it when it refused to come to him.''

Captain Gringo said he was sure sorry the little tyrant didn't know how to treat a lady's pussy; then Estralita left, smiling sort of Mona Lisa. As soon as they were alone, Gaston laughed incredulously and said, "Merde alors, not even a dirty old man like me would risk going sloppiness of seconds to that even dirtier one the poor child sleeps with! Is it not très obvious to you the old bandit suffers from syphilis of the brain, Dick?''

Captain Gringo moved closer to the doorway to make sure nobody was skulking around outside before he growled, "He's not as dumb as she is. But he doesn't add up as what he says he is, either. He has to be older than you, Gaston; and despite the times I've had to call you a dumb bastard, you didn't get that old blustering like a bully ten feet tall for no sensible reason. I give El Chino a 'B-plus' on peasant cunning. He doesn't rate 'D-minus' as a bandit leader.''

"I would not rate his leadership skills that high,'' said Gaston, who'd been in more outfits in his time. Then he said, "Mais if the petty martinet is not what he claims to be, what do you think he really is, Dick?''

Captain Gringo said flatly, "A front man. El Chino's an old con man, not an old guerrilla. He has to be over sixty, and a real halfway successful Nicaraguan bullyboy who'd managed to stay alive that long would be a local legend by this time. We've passed through Nicaragua a lot, and tangled with some real tough Nicaraguan cookies, but do you remember anyone singing songs about El Chino?''

"I agree there seem to be more wheels within the cuckoo clock than any cuckoo we have met so far has mentioned. But this girl at least seems convinced El chino is her adorable Jefe, non?''

"Maybe she and the others aren't as smart as you and me. A front man's supposed to convince everyone he's in command. Did you pick up on that bit about El Chino having an appointment with his *banker*?''

"Oui, but if a guerrilla can call himself a Chinaman, or a cabbage, simple logique would indicate there is no rule forbidding one to call himself El Banquero, non?''

Non. When Estralita came in she didn't tell the old goat a guy called *El* Banquero wanted to see him. She said *your* banker.''

"But Dick, we have been assured by both sides the English branch banks on this side of the river have decamped to the south side avec all their money!''

"Sure. If there was any money on this side of the river to *steal*, these ragged-ass guerrillas would have stolen it and lit out by now. But it may be harder to steal the checking account of a guy with international credit, and did you notice El Banquero didn't seem to notice it was *siesta time*?''

Gaston noddered soberly and said, "Oui! No *Latin* banker would even wonder why business was slow between, say, noon and three or four in the afternoon in Latin America. But the British have always tended to ignore local custom and—Dick, this simply does not add up at all! El Chino was just making dire threats about the colonial funds in the Zion settlement to the south, and he sounded as if he meant what he said about women and children!''

Captain Gringo took out a claro, lit it and blew a thoughtful smoke ring before he admitted, ''I can't add it up either. But let's run through the figures again just for luck. One, on the face of it, El Chino and his followers are simply opportunistic outlaws out to take advantage of the confusion as a British colony goes out of business. But, two, a steamer flying the colors of the British Merchant Marine put in just a few hours ago to unload supplies for El Chino, and I doubt like hell the old goat has a charge account with Marks & Spencer! Three, a harbor-patrol boat, also flying British colors, came putting over to join the fun and games.''

''Mais we did not stay long enough to see what was going on by the waterfront, Dick. How do we know it was an official patrol boat and not a private vessel? Anyone can fly any kind of flag, non?''

Captain Gringo nodded grudgingly and said, ''Good Point. Let's see just what's in those crates the *Trinidad* dropped off.''

Gaston started to follow him across the warehouse. But Captain Gringo hissed, ''Watch the door, you idiot!'' So Gaston did so as the tall American moved in the rest of the way, got out his pocketknife and pried off just enough raw lumber to see what was in the top crate—and whistle. He hammered the board back in place with his gun butt and rejoined Gaston at the entrance, saying, ''He wasn't fibbing about having *machine guns*, anyway. Aside from the one I spotted near the river, there's another back there, still in its factory goo. Did you ever get the strange, sudden feeling you were not alone in the house after all, Gaston?''

Gaston glanced outside and replied, ''There is nobody in our vicinity but us at the moment, Dick.'' But Captain Gringo shook his head and said, ''This outfit has at least one lime-juicer writing checks for 'em. Somebody cleaned a machine gun and set it up by the river between the time we jumped ship and the time I saw it there. We just heard a steam locomotive hauling something somewhere, and natives who know how to run a locomotive don't have to resort to joining guerrillas to get by in the world down here. Any guy with technical skills is in demand. That's why *we* get hired so much by generals who move their lips when they read, see?''

''Mais oui, the old bully admitted he needed followers of some technical ability just now.''

''Bullshit. He's already *got* 'em! I'm not in the mood for unbaked beans right now. Let's see if we can get a closer look at that railroad setup. I didn't know this colony was important enough to have a streetcar line, for God's sake!''

He started out the door. Gaston said, ''Wait. We were just warned not to investigate such matters, and if we do, the other non-hispanic members of this droll group may not like it.''

''I don't like it, either. There's something sneaky as hell going on around here, and I doubt like hell anyone's about to *tell* us what's going on!'' But as he started to press on, Gaston grabbed his arm to swing him around, insisting, ''Pay attention to your sneaky elders, you rash and très noisy youth! I was peeking in convent windows before you were born, and there is always a sneakier way to sneak!''

''Gaston, do you have any idea what you're talking about?''

''Mais oui! Have you forgotten the women we left behind at that house? As I hid them under the roof, I told them to sneak back to their own place and wait for us there, très discreet. By now they may have made it. It would have been safer for them to make a run for it during La Siesta than it will be any minute now, hein?''

''You know where Filipa and her daughter live?''

''Mais non, they told me to just *guess* when I came looking for them. These barrio shacks have no tedious numbers to remember, but Filipa said her casa was behind the farmacia across from La Cantine Azule, so—''

''So what are we waiting for?'' Captain Gringo cut in,

adding; "Let's go, before some guerrilla duty sergeant puts us on KP!"

The two native women had barricaded the door of their two-room alley shack even though none of the guerrillas had quartered in that part of the barrio after all. Once they got the one door clear, they hauled the two soldiers of fortune in and seemed so glad to see them that it seemed impossible either was worried about being raped. They asked them what had happened to the redhead Gaston had left in their charge, and Filipa said Olivia had refused to enter what she referred to as "the nigger quarter." Young Rosalita opined she'd probably gone back to her own house by the church.

Captain Gringo said, "If she did, her husband hasn't noticed yet. He was just over at El Chino's GHQ, bleating for his lost lamb. She could have missed him in passing, I guess, but never mind about her. The guerrillas don't seem to have her, and there are any number of places she could be holed up. The first thing I want you two to tell me about is the railroad here in Gilead. What do you know about it?"

They looked blankly at each other. Then Rosalita said, "What can one say about a railroad, Deek? Los Anglos built it a few years ago for to haul timber out of the jungles to the west. None of us have ever *ridden* on it."

He nodded and said, "Right, short-haul logging line. Probably narrow-gauge, running from the waterfront back to the last mahogany anyone's cut. Have either of you ever heard mention of a Nicaraguan military outpost the rails might make it at least close to?"

This time it was the older native woman's turn to shake her head and say, "Pero no. This has always been a British colony. There are no Nicaraguan settlements of importance in the swamps and jungle all around. A few Indio villages. A few how you say 'squatters' who live off the country and collect chicle for to make Yanqui chewing gum. No town important enough for the central government to even have a post office, though.''

Captain Gringo nodded and told Gaston, ''I *thought* he looked sort of shifty-eyed when he had to come up with artillery in a hurry. He was bluffing about having big guns.''

Gaston shrugged and said, ''You hope. I agree El Chino is not a most convincing military genius; but if he has serious backers, *they* must know what they are up to, and you, my own adorable military genius, are right about a frontal attack against the bigger British settlement being suicidal without some artillery to pave the way!''

Captain Gringo glanced out the small shack's tiny window and said, ''Let's not worry about the plans on this side of the river. They're starting to give me a headache. It'll be getting dark in a few hours. We'll lay low here until it's safe to move out. Then we'll get our tails across to Zion and see if anyone down *there* makes any sense!''

''You intend for to take us with you, do you not?'' sobbed Filipa, throwing her arms around Captain Gringo and pressing him against the wall with her pelvis as she insisted, ''Do not leave us here for the wicked bandits to abuse!''

He said, ''Take it easy. You're getting splinters in my back, only lower down. We'll have to think about that idea some, Filipa. There don't seem to be any guerrillas this far from the center of your barrio, and we may have to fight our way through serious gunslicks between here and the British lines.''

She hugged him tighter, and he had to put one of his own arms around her waist to keep them both from falling as she begged for him to take her and her daughter along. He said, ''For God's sake, nobody's talking about going anywhere before at least six or seven o'clock! Let's just calm down and catch up on our energy between now and then. Do you girls have anything to eat here? The rations the occupation forces issue around here didn't look too inspiring, but we haven't eaten since this morning.''

Rosalita told her mother to stop trying to bump and grind Captain Gringo through the wall of the frame shack as she opened a cupboard to get out some cups and bowls. By the time she'd spread the table—or, in this case, a packing crate—Filipa had calmed down enough for Captain Gringo to pry her loose and join Gaston at the improvised table. The meal that mother and daughter produced in no time would not have rated four stars in Paris, or even Ciudad Juarez. But cold tortillas wrapped around tinned bully beef spiced up with red peppers beat going hungry; and the locally brewed pulque Rosalita poured in their cups wasn't any worse than pulque always was. It served to wash the overspiced grub down, even if it did remind Captain Gringo of mildly alcoholic spit.

The two women said they'd eaten earlier. It was just as well, since there were only two chairs. As they leaned back to light after-dinner cigars, Captain Gringo noticed most of the other serious furniture in this room consisted of a bedroll in one corner. He tried not to think about bedrolls right now. Gaston had no doubt been right about old Estralita being a walking dose of clap, but, damn, those big bare tits had looked inspiring. Filipa had apparently given up on trying to talk her younger male guest into taking them along later, because now she was leaning all over Gaston, telling him no French caballero would wish for to leave unprotected women here at the mercy of banditos. Captain Gringo decided not to think about that, either. Rosalita was making a half-ass effort with the bowls she'd cleared from the table and a bigger pan of battleship gray water on a rickety sideboard. He rose, stepped over beside her and said, "I'd offer to dry if there was any way to *wash* in that greasy crud. Don't you have a well around here?"

She said, "Si, around the back. But my mother is afraid someone will rape me the momento I step outside."

He grinned crookedly, picked up the bowl of dirty dishwater and said he was willing to risk it if she'd get the door. So she held it open for him and he stepped out to dump the crud in the weeds. They could probably use fertilizer as well as water, so what the hell. He moved around to the back of the shack and, sure enough, there was a cast-iron hand pump rising among more weeds. The handle said it had been made in England. It figured. As he pumped the bowl full to overflowing to rinse at least some of the looser grease over the rim, he reflected on the advantages as well as disadvantages of colonialism. This hand pump was an easy example of the advantages the Brits brought to their little brown brothers and sisters, as long as they kept in their own place. He knew that once *this* place reverted to Nicaragua, people like Rosalita would get to carry water from the nearest river on their heads a lot, again. Banana republics didn't go in much for anything but collecting taxes and drafting soldados in out-of-the-way villages like this one. There was a better than even chance that Nicaragua would never do anything at all about Gilead. They had their own problems around the lakes to the west, so why should they bother with a semi–ghost town cut off from the rest of the country by miles of trackless jungle and at least one good mountain range nobody'd built a road through yet either? It seemed a shame that all this work the English colonists and their domesticated natives had put into Gilead would go to waste and be nothing but a memory in a few short years. But there was nothing he could do about it. So he picked up the bowl of now-clear dishwater to lug it back inside.

As he passed a corner of the shack, he heard a woman's voice moaning in agony or ecstasy inside. So he risked a quick peek in the rear window and, yeah, Gaston was up to his usual tricks; and old Felipa, spread out on the floor pallet in the rear room, was acting as if she'd never been eaten before but sure found it something to grin and bear. Captain Gringo muttered, "Bastard. Might have known he'd stick me with the only *virgin* left in town!" as he went on around to the front and shoved the door open with one hip. Rosalita was still standing at the sideboard, blushing a dusky rose, as he put the bowl down for her without commenting on the curtain across the door to the next room or the considerable noise coming from that direction. Rosalita put the bowls from the table into the water to soak, but made no further attempt at washing them as she confided in a whisper, "I think Mother and your friend are doing wicked things in there."

He said, "Well, she did seem anxious to come."

She got it. She giggled and said, "Bueno, *I* like for to come, too, and she would not hear a cannon going off out here right now."

Suiting actions to her unexpected words, Rosalita moved over to her own bedroll, unrolled it across the floor and knelt on it to whip her blouse and skirt off over her head as he just stood there thunderstruck. She looked boldly as well as archly up at him as she knelt there in all her tawny nakedness and asked, "Well? Do you expect me to start without you?"

He grinned, dropped to his knees on the roll beside her and took her in his arms as he whispered back, "aren't we cutting this sort of thin? Your mother's right in the next room, and she seems to think you're some kind of virgin!"

She wrapped her bare arms around him, pressed her firm brown breasts against his still-clad chest and insisted, "Let me show you the kind of virgin *I* think I am. But *hurry*, Deek! We do not have time for all this courting nonsense, Querido!"

That seemed for sure. So he shucked his own duds, fast, as the pretty teenage mestiza lay back smiling sensuously up at him. By the time he'd kicked his pants off, he was feeling sort of sensual too, and she'd told him to cut the bullshit. So he just mounted her like an old friend who didn't expect much foreplay. But she hissed and gave a little whimper of discomfort as he entered her amazingly tight little love box.

He stopped with it halfway in to mutter, "Oh, my God, you really are a fucking virgin!" But Rosalita wrapped her shapely brown legs around his bare buttocks to pull him closer and all the way in as she moaned, "If I got more fucking, I would not be such a virgin. It is most difficult for to get laid when one's mother is always telling hombres not to rob you of your virginity, see?"

He was beginning to. He didn't want to know how many other guys she'd done this with when her mother gave her a few minutes alone with them. As they got down to business, it seemed obvious she'd had *some* practice at this, indeed. So he felt better about what he was doing to such a young kid, and Rosalita liked what he was doing just fine. She came ahead of him, and as he kept pounding she gasped, "Oh, stop, por favor! What if my mother catches us, Deek?"

He told her this was a fine time to worry about that, and as he kept pumping in and out of her post-climactic contractions, she began to move in time with him again and confided she didn't really give a shit if the village priest walked in on them right now.

But it was Gaston rather than the village priest or Filipa who caught them going at it hot and heavy on the floor as he stood in the doorway buttoning his pants. Gaston gulped, ducked back inside, and as Filipa rose from her bedding, buttoning her own blouse, the Frenchman grabbed her, kissed her passionately and lowered her back down to the already messy bedclothing. Filipa gasped, "Querido, what has come over you! I thought we were *through* for the momento!"

Gaston ran an experienced hand up under her skirts as he told her, "Mais non, I thought so too. But for a man of my age, I feel rejuvenated by my lust for your fair flesh, you très adorable creature!"

Filipa giggled as he began to rock the man in the boat between her legs the way he knew she liked it. She said, "Wait, you mad, impetuous Frenchman! My virgin child is in the very next room, and if we do not rejoin them they may wonder what we are doing back here so long!"

He said, "Right now mine feels so long I can't stand it! Let me have just one more orgasm in your divine embrace, my goddess of amour!"

She tried to struggle free. But by this time Gaston's fingers had her love-slicked clit at full attention, so she lay back limply and moaned, "Oh, you are so masterful and I am so weak-willed. But do it fast this time, and let us not take off our clothes again. Rosalita will be wondering what is happening in here, and if she should look in on us . . ."

Gaston assured her he doubted anything like that was about to happen, saying, "I just looked in on them. They seemed very busy with the dishes and, voila, I have it in you again, my proud beauty!"

She gasped, "Madre de Dios, so you have, and it feels as big as ever! How old did you say you were, Querido?"

"A man is as old as he feels, and your little firm body feels as if I am a child molester once more! But could you help me just a bit by moving your adorable derriere, my precious?"

She could, for enthusiastic pelvic movements ran in her family, even if she didn't know it. She might have found out soon, had not Gaston announced loudly in English, "Eh bien! I am coming! I repeat, I am coming, and no doubt we shall *both* be coming all too *soon*!"

So when the two of them were done and Filipa insisted even more firmly on rejoining her virgin child and Captain Gringo, they came out to find Rosalita indeed washing dishes as Captain Gringo dried, trying to look more innocent than he felt. Gaston said, "Ah, there you are. Our hostess and I have just been discussing our escape across the river, Dick."

Captain Gringo said, "I heard. Thanks." And Gaston said, "Think nothing of it. It was my pleasure. Does anyone have the time?"

Captain Gringo said, "Not anymore. It'll be dark enough to move out, soon. Let's talk about that." He turned to the older woman and explained, "As I just told your daughter here, it would be dumb to risk your pretty necks in a firefight at the ford."

"But, Deek! If those soldados find us here—"

"Hear me out, damn it," he cut in, insisting, "In the first place, no guerrillas seem interested in this part of town. They know most of these houses are deserted and stripped bare. So why bother? But if this part of the barrio is too rich for your blood, you still have the deserted English quarter to hide out in, and there are more empty houses in Gilead than there are men in El Chino's army! The place is bigger than we thought."

She said, "Es verdad. But even if the rapists do not find us, what is to become of us if we stay here, Deek? The English people we once worked for are across the river in Zion."

"If they're still there, you mean," he cut in, adding in a

gentler tone: "This colony is going out of business, whether peacefully or not, Filipa. I know it'll be tough on you natives. But there just won't *be* Anglos for you to work for here anymore. Where did you live before Queen Victoria set up shop here?"

Filipa sighed and said, "I have lived here most of my life, and this virgin child here was born in Gilead. I came as a girl from my old village for to work for more dinero, here in the crown colony, see?"

"Yeah, I see. But meanwhile your old village is still out there in the woods somewhere, right?"

"Si, about a day's walk from here on a bay to the north, good for fishing. But how can we go back for to live like peones in a little fishing village where not even the alcalde knows how to read and write, Deek?"

"Easy. You wait till it's dark and start walking. By the time it's light enough for anyone to hunt for you in the jungle, you'll be clear of this mess for good. Don't interrupt me, damn it! I'm thinking of your future, too, and you just don't *have* a future as a housemaid in a British colony these days! If we tried to take you down to Zion we could get you killed, and even if we made it safely across the river, you'd just wind up having to return to your home village within a month or so at the most. So why take chances? Do you want to get this virgin here killed for nothing?"

That worked. Rosalita helped by telling her mother she'd always wanted to meet her grandparents, anyway. So in the end, the sun went down, a guitar started strumming wistfully at what sounded like a safe distance and the two soldiers of fortune were able to take leave of their gracious hostesses without too much of a scene. Gaston got to kiss Filipa *adios*. Captain Gringo didn't think he'd better kiss Rosalita with her mother guarding her virginity again. So as the two of them slipped down the alley in the gathering dusk, he growled at Gaston, "Some guys get all the breaks."

Gaston chuckled and replied, "Age has its privileges, but what are *you* complaining about? As usual, you got the best-looking one!"

•   •   •

There was no hurry in getting to the guarded ford, and guards tended to be most alert when first posted. So, as long as they had time to kill, Captain Gringo insisted on having a peek at the steam locomotive they'd heard that afternoon.

Gaston told him he was going to get them both killed. But it was easier than that. They simply worked their way due north until they came to a narrow-gauge rail line running through the outskirts of the barrio. Then they followed the tracks toward the waterfront.

Since the settlement, while more developed than it looked from the sea, wasn't exactly Kansas City, it only took a few more minutes to reach a modest switchyard; and sure enough, a little Shay logging locomotive stood on a siding up ahead, outlined by the waters of the bay beyond. There was nobody guarding it. But Gaston still said, "Eh bien, now that you have satisfied your curiosity, my cat of nine lives, let us haul ass, as they say in your adorable army. There is no place to go avec the silly locomotive, even if we could get it started, hein?"

Captain Gringo said, "Hell, starting it up would be a snap. The tender's full of wood. Must be green, from the smoke it was throwing before. But once you get a fire going in her box—"

"Sacre goddamn, I shall box your deaf ears in a moment!" Gaston cut in, insisting, "Regard, as I said, there is no place to *go* in the triple-titted machine! To the east the tracks end in très soggy ocean. To the west the tracks may go a few miles into the jungle and then what? If you wish to scamper madly off into the coastal jungles, I shall scamper with you at least as far as the first crocodile-infested swamp. But why leave a trail of steel rails for anyone to follow us, no doubt très pissed off at us for stealing that toy?"

Captain Gringo said, "Relax. I know a colonial lumber line can't take us anywhere important. I'm just doping out the lay of the land where it's sitting. It's hard to tell in this light, but isn't that the tin roof of the warehouse Estralita led us to . . . over there past that pepper tree?"

"It may be. So what?"

"El Chino's schoolhouse GHQ is just beyond it: say, less than a quarter mile. And he probably sleeps in a house when he's not playing school principal. I see why his bimbo didn't want us poking around down this way. There's a cluster of more imposing housing in the angle between the tracks and waterfront. Probably where the guys who used to own this railroad lived."

"Again, so what? We can ask them when we meet them on the safer side of the river, non?"

"Maybe. At least some of these English colonists are up to something I don't think Queen Victoria knows about. El Chino couldn't have had an appointment with his banker down in Zion, and we know old Perkins is still hoping to stay on after the transfer of power. How do we know how many other lime-juicers don't intend to give up all they've worked to build here? Olivia seemed mad as hell about it, and she was *willing* to leave!"

Neither Gaston nor anyone else around there seemed to have any answers for him at the moment. So Captain Gringo glanced up at the quarter moon and said, "Let's go. The guys at the ford have had time to settle down and start swapping dirty stories by now."

They moved back along the tracks until they were well clear of the guerrilla forces camping closer to the waterfront— they hoped—and started working their way south along the dark, deserted streets of Gilead. Again, it didn't take them all that long. But when they saw the river ahead through a gap in the riverside shrubbery, they knew they'd overshot and were too far west.

Captain Gringo said, "Bueno. The last place they'll be expecting anyone from will be the inland jungle side. I don't know how far ahead that guard post is, though. So keep your voice down."

"Merde alors, have I said anything? Lead on, my Mac of Duff!"

Captain Gringo did, and they'd only eased a couple of

city blocks along the rutted muddy lane when they spotted the glow of a night fire ahead. Gaston said, "Eh, bien. They have chosen to make things unusually easy for us. What is the form, Dick? Do we approach très innocent and play our ears on them, or were you considering a cavalry charge?"

"We'll get as close as we can, and take it from there as it comes. And will you keep your voice down, damn it?"

"Poof, we are well out of earshot from the idiots around that très distant fire," Gaston replied, and he was probably right. But their voices had carried at least as far as the house across the road. So Olivia charged out at them, loudly calling, "Is that you, Dick and Gaston! Oh God, I've been hiding all day and I'm so frightened!"

Captain Gringo caught her in his arms and clapped a hand over her mouth as she ran up to him. But the damage had been done. A distant male voice called out, "Hey, did you muchachos hear a woman scream just now?" And then, as the two soldiers of fortune flattened against the bushy riverside vegetation with the redhead now smart enough to quit struggling for Chrissake, they could see the black outline of a guard outlined against the fire's glow as he came up the road, carbine across his chest at port arms!

Shooting him would have been easy. But then what? Captain Gringo growled, "Damn it, Olivia!"

But Gaston had a better idea. He hissed, "Let her stand out in the road in that très feminine summer outfit, Dick. If he does not see *something*, he is only going to keep *looking*!"

Captain Gringo started to object. Then he caught on and told the redhead, "It's the only way. Guys hardly ever shoot even ugly ladies, Red. Are you game?"

She'd caught on too, by now. She gulped and said, "No, but I'll give it a bloody try if you'll make sure he keeps his bloody hands to himself!"

They did. Olivia stepped out in the road, and as the sentry spotted her and stiffened, she called out, "Yoo-hoo, could you tell me where I am, Sir? I seem to be lost!"

The guerrilla lowered the muzzle of his carbine and

came closer as, somewhere behind him, another guerrilla called out, "Hey, Jose?"

The one moving up to meet Olivia called back, "Do not concern yourself on my account, Paco! I have just found some fresh fruit for the picking and I may be a momento or two, eh?"

Actually, he never did return to his comrades around the fire. He moved in on Olivia, stared hard at her in the dim moonlight and said, "Ay, que linda! What is a sweet little thing like you doing in this part of town so late, eh? Are you not afraid of those terrible guerrillas some say are out here at night?"

She asked him to let her pass and, bless her, tried to get around him to his right. So his back was to Gaston as Gaston threw, and the knife went right where the deadly little Frenchman aimed it.

People were not inclined to make much noise after Gaston had his blade in them right. But he still made an awesome thud as he hit the dirt at Olivia's feet, and his carbine clattered even louder as it fell to earth beside him. So the same distant voice called out, "What's going on up there, Jose?"

Olivia gasped, "Oh, dear." But then, she didn't know Gaston was quick with his wits as well as his knife. The Frenchman had been speaking Spanish a lot longer than his version of English, so there was no trace of accent as he called back, "Leave me alone! I'm getting laid!"

It wasn't really a perfect imitation of the late Jose's voice, but the guys down the road all laughed indulgently, and one called out, "Bring her down here when you finish, eh? The corporal of the guard is not due by again for at least two hours!"

So now it was three-on-three, counting Olivia; and now they knew how much time they had. Captain Gringo picked up Jose's carbine as Gaston hauled the body off the road in a hasty attempt at neatness. The American asked the English girl if she knew how to handle a gun. She took it from him, worked the action and said, "Coo, it's not too different from my dad's old hunting rifle."

"Okay, don't spill any more good ammunition working

that bolt and don't fire it unless you have to. Just hang
back and watch what we do, see?''

She said, "I'll try. I'm not sure I'm up to shooting
anyone, though. I've never even killed a deer, and the time
I shot a rabbit made me feel just awful!''

Dames were like that, generally, except the rare individual
who was more bloodthirsty than most men. So he didn't
argue. He led the way, and as they got closer to the
firelight spilling out of the natural archway, moved across
the road to take them at a better angle. Olivia wasn't
supposed to cross with him. But she did, and they were
too close to argue about it now. Captain Gringo stopped
when he got to the edge of the firelight shafting across the
road. Olivia was well back, bless her, and Gaston was in
position to take them from his own vantage from across
the road. So Captain Gringo took a deep breath and braced
himself to do the scary part.

But then, *behind* him, coming along the road leading to
the ford, he heard a distant voice counting out, "Uno, dos,
tres! Uno, dos, tres! Goddamn it, Obregon, you are
supposed to stay in *step!*"

The guards posted at the ford heard it too, of course,
and one of them yelled, "Hey, Jose! Let that puta go and
get back here on the double! El Repollo's out patrolling
again, and you know how picky he can get!''

Captain Gringo started to fade back: there was still time
as the helpful buddy of the late Jose stepped into view to
call him back to his post. But Olivia was sort of new to
night-fighting. So she whipped the carbine stock up to a
dainty shoulder, took dainty deadly aim and, for a lady
who hated to hurt rabbits, blew a lung out the back of the
guy's rib cage pretty good!

Captain Gringo grunted, "Oh, shit!" and stepped out
into the light, gun trained before he'd had time to size up
what he was aiming at. The two surviving guerrillas posted
at the crossing were rising on either side of the machine
gun mounted to face the other way. But their carbines
weren't. So Captain Gringo dropped the closer one first as
Olivia fired again and sent the other ass over teakettle
against the oil drum they'd built their night fire in. It fell

over, spilling hot coals and blazing branches all over the place as Captain Gringo charged in to kick the can of fire, or most of it, into the river just beyond the mounted machine gun. That plunged the gap in the riverside vegetation into darkness—just in time, because other guns were squibbing in the distance now, and those didn't sound like night-flying insects humming through the leaves above and all around!

Captain Gringo snapped, "Gaston, get her across, poco tiempo!" and Gaston didn't argue this time. He simply picked Olivia up, threw her over his shoulder and waded into the river with her still hanging on to her carbine while Captain Gringo dropped to one knee by the Maxim, made sure it was armed, by feel, and yanked it from its mount to rise with it aimed the other way, braced on his hip.

In the distance—not as distant as he'd have chosen if it had been up to him—orange fireflies of muzzle flash were winking at him as blind-fired lead whizzed by all around him, too close for comfort, indeed. He heard the green-sombreroed El Repollo shouting, "Goddamn it, spread out and take cover! Don't stand there in the road like a bunch of bananas waiting for to be plucked!"

That was good enough for Captain Gringo. He fired a long, withering burst of automatic fire into the target area El Repollo had been kind enough to indicate, and from the sound of screams and clattering carbines, he knew he had to be doing *something* right!

But firing at muzzle flashes in a night fight worked both ways. So a whole swarm of angry lead hornets buzzed through the space he'd just fired from, even though he'd been smart enough to crab sideways and brace his other hip against a tree. He let them have another burst, leapt the other way across the clear space—and sure enough, they damned near skinned that tree alive with their return fire. But there didn't seem to be as many of them firing now.

He decided to quit while he was ahead. He backed into the water. It was warm as vomit and didn't smell much better, as he tried to keep his balance backing across a shallow enough but slimy bottom. He knew he could do better if he dropped the heavy weapon. But it still had a quarter of a belt trailing in the water after him. So he hung on to it, straining his eyes as he faced the blackness he'd just left for any movement as he moved even more blindly the other way. It seemed to take forever to cross a ford he didn't remember being that wide. Then a voice behind him called out in English, "All right, you ruddy nigger! We have you covered, so . . . I say, *this* one seems to be a white man too, Sarge!"

Captain Gringo turned around, holding the Maxim at port so they wouldn't mistake him for an unpleasant person; and as he waded the rest of the way, close enough to see what was going on that way, he saw Gaston and the girl standing by the water's edge with a mess of guys in lighter uniforms and pith helmets. As he moved ashore he dropped the Maxim in the grass politely, but muttered, "Wouldn't a ruddy nigger be a contradiction in terms, Constable?"

The constabulary man with the most stripes on his khaki sleeve moved closer to say, "If this other bloke's Fontleroy, you must be the one called Crawford, eh what?"

"That depends on who wants to know. I guess I could be a guy called Crawford, if you'll just stop pointing that revolver at me."

The constabulary sergeant looked down blankly at the big Webley in his fist, said, "Oh, sorry," and put it away as he explained, "All that gunfire has our wind up, I fear. Bad lot on the far side, you know."

"Yeah, we just noticed. Are you two all right, Gaston?"

Gaston called back, "One hopes so. These adorable British police would seem to have been *expecting* us, for some reason."

The sergeant explained, "Oh, rather. We heard a couple of banana chaps called Fontleroy and Crawford had been left behind when a steamer put in on the silly side of the bay and had to weigh anchor in a hurry. We sent a launch over to warn them off this afternoon. They'd already dropped some cargo they'll never see or get paid for, I fear. But her skipper said it was only canned goods. So no real harm done, eh what ?"

"We've been wondering what was going on over there.

Every time we tried to ask, someone pegged a shot at us.
You just heard the last directions they were giving us. The
lady with my friend is Olivia Perkins, she's—''

"Oh, we know the minister and his wife, Sir. Pity he's
being so stubborn about evacuating, but the governor
forbids us to cross over and force our own lot to leave. I
say, is that a *machine gun* you just carried across as well?
The governor will be ever so pleased. We don't have much
in the way of weaponry, you see. The bloody Dons were
supposed to give us time to move out before they moved
in, so we weren't really expecting trouble.''

He turned to order a couple of his followers to pick up
the Maxim. Captain Gringo didn't think they wanted to
argue about whom it might belong to now. So he just kept
his mouth shut and his ears open.

The sergeant said, "Right, Chalmers and Wilson, you
and your rifle squads stay here for now. The rest of us will
escort this lady and these gentlemen to the government
house.''

Captain Gringo didn't think it wise to argue about that,
either; and he had to dry his socks some damned place. So
he fell in with Gaston and the girl as the sergeant and a
few others led them along a barely visible path through an
overgrown patch. They hadn't moved far when they could
see lights ahead. The sergeant said, "The governor will
want a full report before we find quarters for you people.
But it shouldn't take long. He already knows about the
situation on the other side of the river, and as for that
murderer off your ship . . . 'ell, the blighter's stood trial and
been found guilty, so I doubt he'll want you two to give
evidence in a closed case, eh what?''

Captain Gringo frowned and asked him what he was
talking about.

He said, "Oh, didn't you know? Apparently your skipper was keeping it under wraps until he could turn the
culprit over to us on shore. It seems some dago chap
named Romero was murdered the other night aboard the
SS *Trinidad*. Never found his bleeding body, of course.
But they found spots of blood on the deck just outside the
main salon, and that was good enough for the jury. Serious

business, murdering people on the high seas aboard a ship flying the British flag. We'll be hanging the blighter as soon as we have the time. You've no idea how busy we've been in Zion of late.''

Captain Gringo and Gaston exchanged blank looks. Then Gaston asked, ''It sounds too fatigue to endure, Sergeant. But tell me, does this accused murderer of yours have a name?''

The police sergeant nodded and said, ''Of course. Chap called Dodd. D. C. Dodd. Claims to be a man of the cloth, but he has a record as a confidence man and, now, a murderer. But he'll never murder *again*, I'll vow. For we mean to hang him high!''

It was Ladies First at Government House. So Captain Gringo and Gaston got to cool their heels in the waiting room while the royal governor interviewed Olivia first in his office. Staring at the four walls might have been more boring if they'd been in a hurry to meet his nibs. The carpenter's-Gothic building was busting a gut trying to look like a combination of Whitehall and The British Museum, on the cheap. The linen-fold oak-paneled walls of the waiting room were printed wallpaper when you looked closely, and the bench they were sharing was not-too-solid pine. But Captain Gringo wasn't stewing about his personal discomfort at the moment.

He muttered, for perhaps the tenth time, ''I can't let a man hang for a murder he didn't commit, goddamn it! I was in the same spot as Dodd one time. So I know what he's feeling like right now. *Boy*, do I know what he's feeling like!''

Gaston patted the front of his shirt again to make sure he was really out of tobacco before he replied, ''If you intend to turn me in, I wish you would inform me in advance, my conscience-stricken youth. They don't seem to have posted a guard at the exit, and I would like at least a bit of a head start, hein?''

Captain Gringo sighed and said, "You know I can't turn you in. But I can't let that poor slob hang for my crime, either!"

"Merde alors, don't hog all the glory. *I* was the one who stabbed that seductive creature, and one could hardly call it a crime. The annoying mariposa had it coming. His sexual views were disgusting enough; but when one considers he was attempting to blackmail you, as well, what I committed was more what one might call pest control, non?"

"Look, I'm not blaming you for scragging the little shit. I'm just trying to figure out how to keep old Dodd from swinging for it! Doesn't it bother you at all that they've pinned it on the wrong man, Gaston?"

"Mais non. The one they arrested is a species of shit as well. He was a petty criminal, a handler of pans, and a pest."

"I wish you wouldn't speak of him in the past tense. They haven't executed him yet. Why do you suppose the officers of the *Trinidad* hung the execution of Romero on him? Dodd was nowhere near Romero when you and I shoved him over the side."

Gaston shrugged and said, "Merde alors, that is soup of the duck to explain. They put the otherwise useless con man in the frame because he fit it better than anyone else, they thought; and because they had to *frame* somebody to avoid a more thorough investigation once Romero's momma missed him. When the steamer docks at Limon, our adorable skipper simply has to tell the Costa Rican authorities that, while it is true they are missing a passenger named Romero, the matter has been settled, as the accursed killer of the adorable ass-fucker has been arrested for the dirty deed by the British, hein?"

"Yeah, that works. Thanks to our broken-field running with those female passengers, the skipper probably handed Dodd over in good faith as the only one who didn't have an alibi, right?"

"Mais non. I said they framed him, and I meant they framed him. They found no blood on the deck because I was très careful not to *leave* any blood on the deck. So while they knew Romero had gone over the side—a deduction not too difficult to arrive at—they had no idea where or when. Ergo, they simply chose the passenger whose execution would cause the least flapping and turned him over to the police, here. But why am I explaining all this to *you*, of all people? You are in a position to know, better than most, how often people in higher places cover up their own dirty deeds with a hasty frame around the neck of anyone handy, non?''

Captain Gringo cracked his knuckles and growled, ''Don't I ever! Right now the poor bastard's sweating bullets, wondering what the hell he ever did to deserve all this and how come nobody will listen to a word he says! Most of the guys on death row keep insisting it's a bum rap, so the guardo just shrug and keep walking while you beg them through the bars to for Chrissake get you another lawyer!''

Gaston didn't answer. He'd learned long ago it was every man for himself in a wicked world, and he thought it was a sign of weakness to admit feeling shitty when one had to climb over someone else to get to the lifeboats.

The door to their right opened, and a uniformed aide told them the governor would see them now. So they got up and went on in. It was obvious they'd led Olivia out another way, but too obvious a trap for knockaround guys to fall into. They'd decided, as soon as they saw the redhead was going to be interviewed separately, that their stories would have to jibe with hers.

Captain Gringo had expected the royal governor to be a stuffy old country-squire type who pronounced India ''Inja.'' But the man behind the desk was on the pleasant side of forty, kept himself in shape, and the only thing that seemed British Colonial about him was his British junior officer's toothbrush mustache. The aide seated them across the desk from him and discreetly faded out of sight as the governor, whose name turned out to be Forbes, offered them good cigars and waited for them to light up before he said, ''Mrs. Perkins had been kind enough to sketch in the rough outline of your recent adventures, Gentlemen. But there are a few loose strings I was hoping you could clear up for me. Just for the record, of course.''

Captain Gringo did most of the talking as he gave his own version of their day in Gilead, leaving out the dirty parts and sticking to the story that they were a couple of innocent passengers stranded in a guerrilla-held port when their ship left unexpectedly. But he stuck to the truth as far as their actual moves went. So Forbes cut him off when he got to bumping into Olivia again in the dark and said, "Yes, yes, I just assured the poor woman she had nothing to worry about, shooting a couple of the blighters. One could hardly expect white people to sit still for being occupied by bloody dago bandits, and I must say she showed more sense than her husband! I don't know what on earth Reverend Perkins and some of the others who've elected to stay on in Gilead hope to prove. This El Chino sounds like a rum bloke no sensible Englishman could hope to cope with safely. You say the two of you met him personally? I'd like to hear your views on the blighter, since neither we nor our own trustworthy natives ever heard of him and his so-called army of liberation before they popped out of the woodwork like cockroaches a few days ago and, by the way, have you any idea why a Nicaraguan guerrilla leader would try to recruit a couple of banana brokers into his gang?"

Captain Gringo said, "Up front, El Chino struck me as some old jungle-runner they dug up to front for them. He's probably a petty criminal. He may even be vicious, if it doesn't call for risking his own skinny neck. But he's just a stooge."

"The devil you say. Who do you think is behind his deviltry, then, the Nicaraguans who shave more regularly?"

"Nossir. In the first place, the last time we looked, the more important Nicaraguan clans were too busy killing one another to play more complicated games. In the second place, even if we assume there is some Nicaraguan politico, who can read, reading Machiavelli in bed a lot, it still doesn't work. Not even Machiavelli would suggest such a pointless plot. This whole colony's due to be handed over to Nicaragua wrapped in a pink ribbon any day now, right?"

Forbes sighed and said, "I'm afraid so. As soon as we

can manage an orderly evacuation. But it's bloody complicated enough to arrange transportation home for over a
thousand bloody families and all their bloody furniture,
even when bloody bandits leave you alone! Thanks to
those guerrillas lurking just across the river—up to Lord
knows what—most of my constabulary and even civilians
with military experience are tied up pulling rearguard
duty."

He smiled thinly and added, "By the way, you two may
be called on to stand your turns on guard before this is
over. I know neither of you are British subjects. But you
are white men, and I know you both know how to handle
guns. Mrs. Perkins gave quite a glowing account of how
you got her safely to our lines tonight."

Captain Gringo nodded and said, "Your sergeant said
the machine gun we brought with us is the only automatic
weapon on this side of the river right now, and El Chino
has some others."

"So you say. You've yet to tell me why on earth the old
bandit confided so much in two banana brokers he'd never
met before."

"I'm getting to that, Sir. But first we have to work out a
deal."

Forbes looked cautious, but still intellgient, as he asked
his American guest what on earth he meant by *that*.

Captain Gringo said, "To begin with, you can't hang
D. C. Dodd for the murder of Romero."

"The devil you say. He murdered a man aboard a vessel
of British registry. If you're about to point out the late
Señor Romero was a flagrant homosexual, forget it. Dodd
already told us Romero tried to get forward with him and
other passengers, and it put yet another nail in Dodd's
coffin when he was kind enough to supply the prosecution
with his *motive*. I mean, even a homosexual who's not
even an Englishman simply isn't supposed to be murdered
while he's under the protection of the British flag!"

Captain Gringo nodded and said, "Dodd didn't kill the
fruit fly. I can't tell you who did, and I give you my word
it wasn't me. But it wasn't Dodd, and if you hang him I
won't be friends with you anymore."

"Oh dear, I was so hoping you'd come to play in my yard, too. I don't suppose it's occurred to you that as the royal governor here during a military emergency, I have the power to make you do just about anything I bloody want?"

"You have the power, as governor, to pardon Dodd, too. Saves a lot of paperwork. But you're in no position to tell those other guys across the river what to do, and no matter how loud you yell froggy at us, you can't make us jump as high as we might if we put our *minds* to it. You look like an old soldier, Sir. Do I have to tell you the difference between a volunteer and a goldbricker?"

Forbes took another cigar from his desk humidor and lit it as he studied the men across the desk from him a long, thoughtful time. Then he said flatly, "You're not a banana broker, Mr. Crawford. By the way, is that your real name?"

"It's hard to say, Sir. We seem to have lost our ID in all that dashing about behind the enemy lines, and *that* ought to hold up in court, too. But can we cut the bullshit and get down to brass tacks?"

"I wish you would."

"Okay, never mind who we are and you won't have to get writer's cramp explaining things Whitehall doesn't really have to know. As for Dodd, I'll swap you one petty crook for a real mess of big ones if you'll let him go."

"Consider him gone if you can offer *bigger* fish to fry."

"Okay, for one thing, the skipper and at least the senior officers of the *Trinidad* have been running guns to El Chino and his backers. We saw them. They were in the same crates we saw unloaded from the vessel earlier today, and since the steamer flies the British colors, I'd make that High Treason, wouldn't you?"

Forbes started to say something dumb about the quick peek his own harbor patrol had taken at the Gilead quay before getting the hell out of there, fast, with the prisoner the ship's crew had handed over to them. But Forbes wasn't a stupid man. So he nodded and said, "That's up to our Naval Intelligence to prove or disprove. Keep talking. Are you accusing any *other* British subjects?"

Captain Gringo said, "Yessir. Don't have their names for you. But you must know better than me who's chosen to stay on in Gilead and probably here in Zion as well."

"Some of the colonists have seemed rather reluctant to cooperate with the evacuation and, yes, of course we know who most of them are. But refusing to come home when a colony is being turned over to another power isn't High Treason. It's simply bloody silly. Even if they buy El Chino's assurances, what future do they face living here under the perishing Nicaraguan government? Why, dash it all, there *isn't* any Nicaraguan government except on paper. The idiots keep changing governments with their flaming underwear! When we first got word about this colony reverting to Nicaragua, the Grenada forces were in control. But the last I heard, the Leon clique had won this season's civil war and—"

"They know that, Sir," Captain Gringo cut in.

But Forbes looked confused and said, "Well of course they know it. I just said they'd *won* again, damn it!"

"I'm not talking about the Nicaraguans, Sir. I'm talking about some of your colonists. They know the situation here in Bananaland a lot better than London or Washington, since some of them grew up here in this little bit of England on the Mosquito Coast. They know nobody in Nicaragua's too interested in this neck of the woods in the first place, and that any Nicaraguan officials who might ever show up would be easier to bribe than a British colonial official."

"See here, Sir, I'll have you know I've never taken a bribe in my bloody life!"

"That's what I just said, Governor. Public officials aren't paid as well in Latin America. Even if they thought they'd have more trouble making a buck or, let's say a pound, under Nicaraguan jurisdiction, a lot of them would still think it was worth a try. This little colony's been run on the cheap by Her Majesty. So she can afford to forget her modest investment and, hell, probably save money on flags and office paper if she just lets go. But the colonists who've done the work of *colonizing* this coaling station your Royal Navy grabbed by reflex action back in the forties have a lot more to lose. All the housing and business construction I've seen so far—save for this cheap government house here—was built with other people's time and money. Hell, the quay up at Gilead was imported cobblestone and someone even built a *railroad* there.''

"Yes, the Gilead Lumber Company, Limited, and...hmm, are you suggesting British subjects would turn their backs on their own mother country just because they didn't approve of current British policy on this side of the water?''

Captain Gringo laughed and said, ''No offense, Sir. But that's a mighty stupid question to ask a Connecticut Yankee! I had an ancestor who fought at Lexington Green the day some other British colonists decided London was giving them the shaft. I'm not sure I approve of the methods *this* bunch of pissed-off colonists seems to have in mind. For one thing, they could be playing with fire. But I'm not sure I can fault them for wanting to hang on to the good things they had going for them here.''

''A man who'd turn his back on his own mother country simply couldn't be considered a gentleman. But come to think of it, we do seem to get a rather rough lot going out to the colonies to seek their fortunes. What was that you said about playing with fire?''

Captain Gringo explained, ''Knowing Great Britain was abandoning them, and probably not too keen on becoming Nicaraguans overnight, some wise-asses have imported El Chino and his thugs to front for them. They already have the northern settlement of Gilead completely under their control.''

''The devil you say. Gilead's been occupied by Nicaraguan guerrillas. If it was up to me, we'd get some Royal Marines in here and clean the buggers out. But Whitehall says not to bother, because—''

''Because London thinks it would be silly to spill blood and money over real estate they're letting go of,'' Captain Gringo cut in.

Gaston, who'd been trying to keep quiet and let him do all the talking, but was finding it painful, said, ''Merde alors, I had not one species of ancestor at Lexington, and even *I* can see the plan! The sly dogs backing El Chino mean to move you off the property sooner than planned, forcing you to abandon almost everything but your adorable asses, you are supposed to think, to guerrillas. Then, once you are gone, voila, the brave Englishmen who elected to stay on will simply rise and chase the unwashed balls of grease back into the bushes, to no doubt proclaim Mission Bay an independent democracy, avec the full approval of Washington and no doubt total indifference of Nicaragua, hein?''

Forbes started to object, chewed his cigar instead and said, ''Barstards! It will probably work, too! The Monroe Doctrine says nothing about local populations setting up their *own* new governments down here! If it did, the persishing U.S. Marines would never get to see their families! But what can London do about this dastardly plot?''

''Not much,'' said Captain Gringo. ''That part of it would sit well with Washington and wouldn't hurt either Britain or Nicaragua all that much. But I'm not sure the colonists secretly backing El Chino have thought it all the way through. That's why I said they were playing with fire. It's easy enough to pay a mess of local bandits to come and occupy you so you can rebel against them and run up your own new flag. But there can't be more than a handful of Englishmen in on the plot or we wouldn't have seen so many empty houses up in Gilead. They think they're controlling El Chino and his thugs. They may be, for the moment. But El Chino does have an army now, thanks to them being so cute; and the old goat has his eye on the money down here in your vaults. He was acting pretty independent about some Englishman who wanted to chat with him this afternoon, too.''

Forbes gasped and said, ''Oh, good Lord, we have all the money from all the banks in the colony under lock and key downstairs, too! But even if the traitors who brought this plague upon us all can't control their unwashed Frankenstein creation, we only have to hold out until our transports arrive, and in a pinch, I could still cable for a detachment of real troops.''

"Sure, but how much time are we talking about, Governor?"

"Let me see. . . . A convoy of passenger steamers are due in less than a week, and they should at least be able to take off most of the women and children."

"Yeah, and if you cabled tonight for the Royal Marines, it would take 'em, what, at least two *more* weeks to get here?"

"If Whitehall dispatched them right away. Naturally they'd have to study the matter and—"

"And El Chino was talking about hitting you before you can get the women and children off!" Captain Gringo cut in, adding: "Thanks to the Englishmen working with him, he knows more about your defenses and plans than we know about his! He said something about getting his hands on some artillery. I hope he was bluffing. He may have expected us to make a run for it and tell you what we've just told you. But on the other hand, he didn't strike me as a chess master, and they did try pretty hard to keep us from crossing the lines. So let's call the odds fifty-fifty on that. If he starts lobbing shells into Zion, you'll just have to give in to him. There's an outside chance you can hold him off if he's planning to come at you the *hard* way."

Forbes objected, "Nonsense! It would be suicide for them to attempt a crossing if all they have is small arms!"

Captain Gringo shrugged and said, "*We* made it across without too much trouble tonight, and one of us was a sissy girl."

"Yes, but my men had the drop on you lot as you waded ashore, if you'll remember."

"I do. Like I said, there was only three of us, and you had no more than a squad or more of constabulary to stop us. What if there'd been a hundred or more of us firing from the hip as we came?"

"Well, there wasn't; and thanks to you, we have a machine gun to set up there as well, eh what?"

"If it's chambered for your ammunition, Sir. I used up most of the belt on my way out. I'd better have a closer look at that Maxim. If it's chambered for thirty-thirty—and that's what most guns fire in this neck of the woods—

lots of luck! I couldn't help noticing your constabulary was armed with Enfields, and they don't take Yankee ammo rounds worth shit!''

That part turned out okay. Governor Forbes got them down to the guardroom fast as hell, and to everyone's relief, the British-made Maxim was chambered to fire British ammo after all. It figured British gunrunners would run British guns to Nicaraguan gunslicks, as soon as you studied on it some. As Captain Gringo checked the machine gun out, Gaston asked Forbes if he had any heavier weapons on hand at all. Forbes said, ''Well, we do have one four-pounder to fire salutes with. But I fear all our ammunition is blank. It's just not considered cricket to fire on vessels entering the harbor with anything more serious.''

Gaston sighed and said, ''Eh bien, that is what I feared you would tell me, M'sieu. I am très formidable with a field gun, but I have never been able to hit anything important with a blank round; and naturally your adorable little sunset gun will have been mounted as usual on a stationary post?''

Forbes said, ''Naturally,'' and Gaston muttered, ''Merde!''

Captain Gringo snapped the action of the Maxim shut and opined, ''Well, if I can get somebody to help me stuff this one belt with fresh ammo, that would mean one belt at least to work with.''

Forbes asked if he thought that would be enough, and he said, ''No. This soggy belt holds no more than two hundred rounds, and a machine gun fires six hundred rounds a minute. Add it up, Sir.''

Forbes did, grimaced and said, ''I'll see if our ordnance men can improvise more belts out of canvas. It doesn't look too complicated. How many machine-gun belts are we talking about, Mr. Crawford?''

''At least a dozen. By the time they're used up, we'll have stopped them or it won't matter. It all depends on how dumb and brave they are, see?''

"No, I fear I don't see! Surely no mere guerrilla band could stand up to so much automatic fire as you're suggesting, Sir!"

Captain Gringo growled, "Suggesting it, hell, I'm *telling* you one machine gun could probably hold one section of the line long enough to matter. If they begin their attack with an artillery barrage or cross upstream to hit us from another direction, it's been nice knowing you!"

"I say, how could they get across anywhere but the ford? The water's over ten feet deep, a good twenty miles inland!"

"Is there a law saying a guy wouldn't rather walk twenty miles upsstream than charge a machine-gun emplacement head-on, Governor? They might not do it that way. They have a whole empty town to work with, mostly made out of wood; and the last time I looked, wood still floated the same as always!"

Forbes grimaced and said, "You do paint a pretty picture, don't you?" Then he took out his pocket watch, looked down at it and said, "Well, I doubt from what you've told me they intend to attack tonight, and it's perishing late. Perhaps we'd all better sleep on it and see if things don't look brighter in the morning. You two will want to stay here at Government House for now. The only decent hotel in Zion's been boarded up, even if it wasn't too far for me to get my hands on you in a hurry, eh what?"

Neither of them asked just how he meant that. They didn't want to know. So the governor led them outside, found an aide who didn't seem to be doing anything more important and told him to show the soldiers of fortune up to the guest rooms on the top floor.

The aide did, and things began to look brighter already. Captain Gringo and Gaston each got his own cozy room under the mansard roof of corrugated iron. The somewhat Spartan quarters were clean, and both the walls and bed linens were white. As soon as they were alone in the room assigned to Gaston, Gaston murmured, "Eh bien, you got Dodd's neck out of the noose without putting ours in it.

But from that point on you lost me! You were shitting the bull about us helping them hold out here, non?''

Captain Gringo shook his head and said, ''We have to. We have no other choice. The only way we could get out of here without a boat is on foot through soggy country infested with civil war as well as snakes.''

''True, but we have managed to wade through snakes and civil wars before, non? We *could* step on a snake if we just started running now. We *could* stumble into other noisy people in a country where noise seems to be the national sport. Mais if we stay *here* we are *certain* to trade shots with El Chino's pirate crew!''

''We just did, and we came out all right, didn't we?''

''Oui, another reason I never wish to meet El Chino again, Dick! One tends to doubt he likes us as much, now, and he still has at least three more machine guns to play with than you do, as good as you are!''

''Screw the automatic weaponry. Is there any chance you could improvise some sort of warheads for that sunset gun? I've never forgotten the time you fired tomato cans out of an old cannon.''

Gaston chuckled, but said, ''Oui, that was très amusé. But that time I had a smoothbore Spanish cannon and black powder to work with. To fire anything worth lobbing up the rifled bore of a four-pounder, with cordite, requires considerable forethought as well as caution; and if we had that much *time,* we would not need a big gun in the first place, Dick!''

Captain Gringo said, ''Forbes was right. We're too tired and talked-out to think clearly. Hit that sack and think on it. I'll be right next door if you need me.''

''Merde alors, do I look like that kind of a boy?''

Captain Gringo laughed and went next door. He sat down and hauled off his boots. He was mildly surprised to find his socks were still wet. It felt like longer than that since they'd forded the Mission River with Olivia. He wondered where the redhead was right now. Probably staying with friends here in Zion. He wondered why he wondered about redheads when he felt so bushed. He wondered why he had a semi-erection when he stripped all

the way and gave himself a quick whore bath with a
washrag and the water basin on a sideboard. Then he
flipped off the Edison bulb and climbed into bed. The
mattress on the iron bedstead was a little Old School—firm,
but the clean sheets felt delicious against his naked skin
and, Jesus, it would be good to get a good night's sleep
after the rough day he'd just had.

So he'd have been mighty pissed off to have anyone
come in to ask if he was still awake, if it had been anyone
but a luscious redhead wearing nothing but the chemise
she'd left home with under her more sedate Gibson girl
outfit.

There was just enough light coming in from the street
lamp out front to show him she had let her red hair down
to frame her beautiful face like a church window as she
calmly proceeded to climb in bed with him, explaining,
"I've been waiting up here for hours, it seems."

He made room for her with his hips, but took her in his
arms as he grinned and answered, "Me too. I was afraid
you'd gone to stay with friends, and Governor Forbes sure
is turning out to be one hell of a friend of *mine*!"

He started to kiss her. Olivia turned her face away and
said, "Wait, Dick. A few ground rules, first. I have no
friends to stay with here in Zion. Its mission was started
by bloody Mormons, and we Congregationalists don't talk
to them."

"Who cares? You *have* a friend to stay with, here and
now!"

She didn't object to his hand on her breast, which felt
even better than expected, but she said, "I'd better tell you
I'm a faithful married woman before we go any further,
Dick."

He frowned at her and said, "Oh, sure you are. Anyone
can see that. Can we get this chemise off, Doll? Jesus,
you're built!"

She said, "Stop that. We have all night for sex, Dear. I
just want to explain my position, first."

"What's the mattter with the missionary position, at
least to start? You're a missionary, aren't you?"

"I'm a missionary's wife, and I don't intend to leave

Hiram, ever! We were married in church and he's been a good husband to me, in his fashion. So I'll let you have me, but I want no nonsense about me running away with you afterwards, see?''

He was beginning to. He smiled at her incredulously and asked, ''Are you afraid I'll wind up proposing to you, for God's sake?''

And she sniffed. ''Coo, it happens all the time. Some of you men just can't seem to understand how a woman with, well, her own needs, can still feel true to her husband in her own way.''

He nodded and said, ''Yeah, he did seem a little old for you, come to think of it.'' And she said, ''Don't be beastly. I'll not have you talking behind my husband's back, Dear. It's not Hiram's fault that he simply, ah...can't get it up anymore.''

He was up pretty good, himself, right now. So he said, ''Right. I get the picture. We're not cheating on your husband. We're just going to fuck.''

Olivia sniffed indignantly and said, ''Hoy, watch your bloody language! I'll have you know you're talking to a fucking lady!''

He sure was, once he'd kissed her to shut her up and mounted her to get in her as best he could with that damned shift in the way. Olivia moaned, ''Oh, that feels loverly, Dick! I had no idea you were so tall! And you may be right about this bloody chemise!''

So he worked it off up over her head as she bumped and ground under him, and as he settled back down against her lush, naked torso, she wrapped both her arms and legs around him to sob, ''Coo, it does feel ever so much nicer, stark bloody bare. But please don't get carried away and tell me you love me while we're coming, Dear!''

He laughed and said, ''Hey, who's excited?'' as he proceeded to screw her silly. Thanks to his earlier adventure on the kitchen floor with little Rosalita that same day, he was able to keep going longer than she was probably expecting, since even a grown man would tend to come quick as a schoolboy in anything as nice as this. But thanks to how nice it was, he had no intention of even slowing down in the foreseeable future. Olivia was a fantastic lay as well as a real looker, in or out of her clothes. So the results were most pleasing to both of them. She purred, "Oh, I love your stamina, Dick! Not *you*, mind; it would be wicked for a girl to love any man but her husband, but . . . Jesus, if only Hiram could do me like this even once a bloody month . . ."

He didn't want to hear about her in bed with other men, whether they could do her right or not, and it would have been rude as hell to comment that any man who could sleep with such great company and do it less than once a month to her had to be sick as well as old. He was pretty sure he could come in her skilled, pulsating snapper with a bullet in his head. But it felt even greater to ejaculate in her, hard, while he was wide-awake and she—from the way she was moving her trim hips—was even more so.

She sighed and said, "Oh, rats, I feel your love juice running down the crack of me arse, and I was almost there!"

He didn't answer. He kept moving it in and out of her. It was easy. She felt even better inside, now, tight with pending orgasm and slicked with both their juices. She must have liked it too, because she suddenly sobbed, "Oh Lord, strike a bloody light, I'm really . . . comingggggggg!"

She sure was, and he wanted to, so he started pounding harder as Olivia gasped, "Coo, give a girl a chance to catch her bleeding breath, you animal! I'm too sensitized and you've got me so excited I'm . . . oh, oh, yesssssssss!"

He seemed to have created a monster, once he'd brought her to full climax the first bashful time. For she beat him to his own climax with yet another of her own, and when he finally came in her the second time, she had her nails dug into his buttocks and was begging him not to stop, not to ever stop, and even moaned some words of love her husband might have been upset to hear.

But when he rolled her on her hands and knees to see if a change of position would inspire him to new greatness, or at least keep him going in the insatiable redhead, Olivia murmured conversationally, "I didn't really mean that—about not ever having such a loverly dong up me before, I mean. There's nothing I love better than my own true lover's dong, if only he could put it in me more often.''

He didn't answer. He was getting tired of her silly game, even if her pale derriere wasn't boring him at all as he watched himself going in and out between its soft cheeks in the soft light, dog-style.

She giggled and murmured, ''Oh, this feels so wicked, even if it does feel loverly. I'm not sure the church would approve of this position, do you, Dick?''

He said, ''Let's not tell anyone, then. Ah, could you arch your spine a bit more, Doll?''

She could and did, saying she was so glad he understood thtat nobody was ever to know about what they were doing, since some might not understand. He assured her as he screwed her that he understood her position perfectly. So she suggested they try some other positions; and for a man who'd intended to get a good night's sleep, Captain Gringo got hardly any that night. But in truth he had no complaints. A guy could always catch up on his sleep alone, and she said sleeping alone was a perishing bore, too.

From the way she was keeping him awake, Olivia had been doing a lot of that lately.

She slipped out before dawn, of course, warning him she'd just never forgive him if he breathed a word about her odd vicws on marital fidelity to a living soul. So he promised, and having promised, saw no point in even telling Gaston when they had breakfast together downstairs in the constabulary mess. The governor wasn't there. They didn't ask where he ate breakfast. They didn't care. They washed down their awful rations with pretty good tea and went out to explore the situation on this side of the river.

They found a waterfront bar open, asked a few questions as they inhaled some gin and tonic, then strolled around the slightly larger settlement of Zion without learning much they could use to keep the guerrillas out of it.

Like Gilead across the river, Zion had begun as a missionary outpost, in this case one established by English Mormons. Neither the Latter-day Saints nor the Congregationalist missionaries who'd set up shop across the river—albeit on the same handy natural harbor—had asked either Nicaragua's or Great Britain's permission in the beginning. The few local Indians had been happy enough about the food and medicine their mysterious paleface friends from who-knew-where were willing to provide. But it was up for grabs how many of them took the religious messages that went with the good stuff seriously. Those few Indians who knew anything at all about Christian teachings tended to be lukewarm Roman Catholics while, naturally, the more assimilated Nicaraguan mestizos or Spanish-speaking breeds along the Mosquito Coast considered themselves pure Spanish Catholics, no matter how much their Indian bloodlines showed. For some reason, Moravian missionaries farther up the coast seemed to have more luck turning Mosquitos into nominal Protestants; and neither Zion nor Gilead had ever amounted to much until, during the coastal gunfights of the 1840s, the Royal Navy had claimed the bay in the Queen's High Name as a handy coaling station. Before setting up the coal tipples, of course, they'd gone through the pro forma bullshit about having to protect English missionaries and poor downtrodden Indians even though, up until now, nobody else had seemed too interested—and probably still wouldn't have been too interested—had not the official government setup caused the place to just grow like Topsy. Now that the Royal Navy had no further use for the place, of course, everyone from honest businessmen to the whores and gamblers who always followed the fleet had a lot to lose if El Chino took over.

The housing on this side of the river was occupied and then some. Only a few civilians from either settlement had been evacuated in the early confusion, and so many families who'd fled Gilead were bedded down with friends, relations or sudden landlords on the south side of the river. At least two-thirds of the natives who'd fled the Gilead barrio were camped on this side as well—less comfortably than the English, of course, but they were used to that; and at least the disciplined constabulary was less likely to mistreat them than their fellow countrymen swaggering around Gilead under El Chino or whomever he worked for. Native Nicaraguans probably knew the local guerrilla customs better than anyone else, and it was a sobering thought to see so many of them had voted with their feet to stay with the English as long as they could. Sobering, too, was the sight of so damned many kids playing on the dirt streets of Zion no matter what their mothers said about their getting dirty. It was impossible to keep kids inside on a sunny tropic morning, and as Gaston observed, they were just as safe out-of-doors as inside a frame house if El Chino wasn't bluffing about the big guns he was expecting.

They found the only cannon Zion had mounted, as expected, on a post overlooking the harbor near the customs house. Gaston opened the breech and peered up the tube, muttering, "Eh bien, spick-and-span as one would expect English gunners to keep it. Mais regard how some triple-titted dimwit has welded it in place!"

"It can't be traversed at all?" asked Captain Gringo.

Gaston slammed the breechblock back in place and replied, "Mais non, it can't even be elevated or depressed. One suspects that in the interest of avoiding accidents, some doer of too much good made cetain it was only good for firing salutes due east at the open sea at a thirty-degree angle, forever!"

"What if we cut the gun out of its mounting?"

"Avec what, Dick? That is solid steel, très hardened by welding that, for all we know, took the temper out of the breech as well! It is one thing to fire blank rounds from a species of scrap iron like this. Nobody with the brains of a gnat would risk his adorable ass by bringing a real H.E. round anywhere *near* that breech, hein?"

As they stood there morosely regarding the useless piece of ordnance, a rather officious constabulary sergeant they hadn't met yet marched up to them and said, "Hoy, you blokes, what do you mean by mucking about with Her Majesty's property?"

Gaston snorted in disgust and replied, "You mean

someone *owns* this très ridiculous gun? We thought some
child had dropped it.''

''You're not to touch it again, unless you want to
answer to the governor for it, eh?''

Captain Gringo put a possessive hand on the four-
pounder to help make his point as he said, ''We've already
talked to the governor about it, Sergeant. Now I want you
to gather a work detail for me. Better scout up a couple of
hacksaws and plenty of spare blades, too. Dismounting
this gun's going to be a bitch, but it has to be done. So
carry on.''

The burly noncom blinked in astonishment and said,
''Coo, not bloody likely! You must be off your chump if
you expect me to damage government property!''

Captain Gringo insisted, ''It's already damaged. Some
asshole welded it in a fixed position, pointing out to sea;
and those guerrillas are up *that* way, see? I want you to
saw it loose. It's going to take some time, so I'll get back
to you in, let's see, about two hours. That ought to give
you time to saw through the welds, don't you agree?''

''I bloody do not, whoever you think you are! Who in
the blinking hell *do* you think you are? You're no ruddy
officer! Why, damn it, I don't even think you're British!''

Captain Gringo nodded pleasantly and said, ''I'm not.
But if you don't have this gun dismounted for me when I
get back here in two hours, you can commend your soul to
Jesus, Sergeant, because your *ass* will belong to me! Let's
go, Gaston. I have some other guys to chew out at
Government House if they haven't whipped up those
machine-gun belts I ordered yet!''

He marched grandly away with Gaston tagging along,
trying not to laugh until they were out of earshot. When
they were, the Frenchman said, ''Eh bien, I doubt they can
saw through in two hours, but I do admire your way with
noncoms, Dick. Was there any point to all that back there,
or were you just handing back the shit of chickens to the
species of martinet?''

Captain Gringo said, ''If we can mount the tube on
some sort of improvised gun carriage, it ought to at least
look like a serious fieldpiece, right?''

"Perhaps, but I forbid you as a kindly old artilleryman to even consider *firing* the damned thing! I am très serious, Dick. Trust a man who knows something of bursting breeches! We killed more of our own gunners than the Boche we were aiming at, at Sedan, thanks to French war profiteers I hope the Boche robbed très thoroughly when he marched into Paris in seventy!"

Captain Gringo nodded and said, "I've seen cannon fire sideways instead of the way they were aimed. Messy. But what the hell, we don't have any real ammo to fire from that four-pounder, so quit your bitching. Half the battle's bluff in these sieges, and how in the hell is the other side to know an empty cannon from a loaded one, pointed point-blank across a ford at them?"

"Ah, I see the method in your madness. But what if they *call* your bluff, Dick?"

"We'll still have that Maxim and other guys on our side with their own bolt-actions. I thought you were going to quit your bitching."

"Mais non, I've barely started! El Chino is not after you and me, personally. If he comes across, it will be to get at the *money* on this side of the river. What if we were to simply go for a stroll in the forest, say, down at the far end of this town of one horse, and when it was all over—"

"A lot of horses could be dead, along with a lot of women and children," Captain Gringo cut in. So Gaston contented himself with another Merde Alors and went into a silent sulk as they moved up the waterfront together.

They hadn't gone far when a familiar voice called out, "Hey, you guys, I've been looking all over town for you since they cut me loose this morning?"

It was the fake minister and full-time con man, Dodd, of course. He ran up and tried to shake both their hands at once as he told them how grateful he was for their getting him out of jail. He said, "I thought, I say I thought, I was a goner for a time there, gents! Those rascals from the steamer railroaded me just awful, and don't anybody, I say anybody, try to tell you these lime-juicers give a man a fair day in court! Sweet Jesus, gents, I've stood many a trial on many a charge and I have never seen a hearing go that fast! It seemed they'd no sooner frog-marched me over here from that other place than some rascal in a goat-hair wig was telling me I was about to hang by the neck until dead...dead, I say, *dead*! How did you sweet-talk me out of that fix, Son?''

"Easy. I just told them you didn't do it. Are you any good with a gun, Dodd?''

"Me, a man of the cloth, I say the *cloth,* with a *gun*? Surely you must be joshing me, Son.''

"No I'm not, Rev. If I call you 'Rev,' will you cut the other bullshit? You probably missed out on a lot that was going on across the bay and I haven't time to tell you the whole tale. Suffice it to say the guys who tried to get you hung for one of the few things you weren't guilty of were running guns over that way to worse guys than *any* of us. They may be heading this way, any time, with said guns. So are you in or out, Rev?''

"The bastards who tried to frame me, I say *frame* me, are looking for a rematch, Son? I'm in, of course. I wouldn't want this to get around, you understand, but before I saw the light and took up the spreading of the light, I, ah, used to be pretty handy with the, ah, devil's tools.''

Captain Gringo nodded and said, "I figured you for an old gunslick when I couldn't help noticing the way you dealt cards aboard the schooner. Nobody who cheats that brazenly could have made it to middle age unless he was able to take care of himself in sudden saloon emergencies. Stick with us. We're on our way to the governor now, and they've got plenty of rifles there. They just don't have enough good shots to issue them all to.''

But as it turned out, they didn't get to the government house right away, after all. It was in sight, ahead, when one of the khaki-clad officers they'd met the night before ran up to them, out of breath, to gasp, "I've been looking all over for you lot!''

"There seems to be a lot of that going on this morning. What's up, Lieutenant?''

"A parley at the river crossing. Chap in a big green hat

says he's a friend of yours and that he has a personal message for you to give that redhead of yours, Crawford.''

Captain Gringo grunted. "Shit, I was hoping I'd hit El Repollo. And Olivia Perkins is not anyone's redhead but her husband's. But, okay, leg's go see what our little green cabbage wants.''

They found El Repollo and another guerrilla holding a dirty white flag talking to Governor Forbes and some other colonial officials on the Zion side of the river crossing. On the far side, other guerrillas stood casually about with their carbines cradled. That was fair. Forbes had plenty of constabulary covering him too, as he stood by the water's edge with El Repollo.

As Captain Gringo joined them, the green-hatted mestizo smiled at him pleasantly enough, considering, and said, "El Chino *thought* that was you who smoked us up last night, Captain Gringo. Was that any way for to treat friends who were willing to cut you in on the loot?''

Captain Gringo said, "Never mind the bullshit. You say you have a message for Olivia Perkins?''

El Repollo took a wadded-up sheet of stationery from the pocket of his green shirt and handed it over, saying, "Si, her husband, the late Hiram Perkins, wrote it to her before we shot him this morning. El Chino said for to bring it with us, for to discover if it really was you and this little Frenchman who helped her escape. He had other plans for the sweet young thing, and now he will have plans for you as well. But I do not think El Chino means to fuck *you*, you gringo bastard!''

Governor Forbes gasped. "I say, did you really execute poor Reverend Perkins? Whatever for, you brute?''

"Hey, don't call a nice kid like me names under a flag of truce, eh?'' El Repollo grinned, and went on to explain, "It was not my idea for to shoot the old bastard, even if he *was* a Protestant. But as our great leader says, one has to start with *someone* to prove a point; and what *else* was Perkins good for?''

Captain Gringo told him to shut up as he unfolded the note and read:

Dear Heart: By the time this reaches you, I fear I shall be with my maker. But try to be a brave girl and do not grieve for me. I go to my Eternal Salvation secure in the knowledge I have done my best as a Soldier Of The Lord and, Dear Olivia, these last few years with you have been more reward than most men ever dream of. But you know how I feel about you, My Beloved. So now, in hopes of them delivering this last good-bye for me, I must digress a bit and tell you what this distressing El Chino person has directed me to tell the royal governor.

Captain Gringo swallowed and handed the note to Forbes, saying, ''I think this part's meant for you, Sir. I'm not sure we ought to show this note to the widow Perkins. They just let him write it to get some kind of other message across!''

Forbes quickly scanned the crumpled sheet and gasped, ''Oh, I say, you're all too right! They've rounded up all the colonists who chose to stay behind when we evacuated Gilead, and now the blighters mean to shoot them one by one, beginning with poor old Perkins, unless I give in to their demands!''

He handed the note back to Captain Gringo to do with as he may and turned back to El Repollo to demand, ''Very well, my good fellow, just what are these demands of your rebel leader?''

''Hey, watch that *rebel* shit, Gringo! Do I look like an Englishman? I am Nicaraguan, damn your eyes, so for how could I rebel against your puta of a queen even if I wished to, eh?''

''Never mind all that! You say you mean to shoot your captives who *are* British subjects unless certain demands are met. One can hardly meet demands before one *hears* them, dash it all!''

El Repollo grinned like a mean little kid and said, ''I

think you know what we want, Señor Gobernador. You can keep your ugly women. We do not even want your pigs and chickens. We just want the *money* you have locked in your vault for safekeeping. Is that too much for to ask?''

''You're bloody-ass right it is!'' gasped Forbes, adding: ''That money was placed under the protection of the Crown, and that's where I mean to keep it if you don't mind!''

El Repollo laughed and said, ''Hey, *I* don't mind if you shove it up your ass, Señor Gobernador. But El Chino says if you do not wish for to hand it over gracefully, he may just have to kill some pigs and chickens after all, eh? Did you read that part Perkins wrote about the guns we have for to do it with?''

Captain Gringo hadn't. So as Forbes went on trying to reason with the unreasonable El Repollo, he scanned over the part about other hostages and read, near the bottom of the page:

I fear these bandits have managed to obtain some field artillery pieces from somewhere, Dear Heart. I know little of such matters, but they just took me over to the rail yards; and while I can't say what sort of guns they are, they have four of them and, oh yes, El Chino says to tell the governor they are French 75's, whatever that means. The people holding me refuse to listen when I tell them I know the governor will never give in to their demands whether they shoot me or not. So I imagine they'll be coming for me any minute now. In closing, let me only add that you and my English friends may wish to give a mass for my soul; and as you know, my favorite psalm has always been Jeremiah 8:22, and that the refrain, of course, is still *Nay, Nay, Never!*

Perkins had started to write something else. But apparently they'd stopped him at that point, satisfied he'd gotten their intended message across and not giving a damn what a man who was about to die intended to say to his wife. They hadn't even let the poor old guy sign it.

Captain Gringo put the note away and tried to pick up

on what Forbes was saying to El Repollo. The green-hatted bandit didn't like it much. So he said, "We waste time, here. I must go back and tell the others you are not a reasonable person. Think the matter over while you still have time, eh? We are not bad guys. We do not wish for to shell a village crowded with women and children. But unless you hand over the money, you give us no other choice."

He nodded to his standard-bearer and turned away. Then he had an afterthought and turned back again to tell Forbes, "By the way, do not think you can trick El Chino by turning over just *some* of the money. We know to the centavo how much you have in your vault. An English banker over in Gilead was kind enough to tell us when we asked most politely, with a gun to his head."

El Repollo turned away again to splash back across to the other side. Forbes murmured, "You were right, Crawford. They have created a monster they no longer control! But the men they've seized are still British subjects, dash it all. So what are we to do?"

Gaston suggested, dryly, "Let the bandits shoot them, of course. Children who play with matches deserve to get burned, and it saves you the expenses of all those trials, hein?"

Forbes shook his head and insisted, "Her Majesty's Government doesn't work that way, Fontleroy. Nobody is allowed to execute British criminals but a British hangman, after a fair trial and all that."

Then he shot an odd look at Captain Gringo and asked, "By the way, ah, Crawford, why did that chap just call you Captain Gringo instead of Crawford?"

Captain Gringo was afraid the bastard had been listening sharp. He shrugged and replied, "Beat me. He called *you* a gringo too, remember?"

"Yes, but not *Captain* Gringo. There's only one bloke I've ever heard of who answers to that name in this part of the world, and . . . by Jove, you fit the description on those Wanted fliers the U.S. Justice Department was kind enough to send us, too. You're not . . . ?"

"Do you really want to know?" sighed Captain Gringo

as Gaston added with a sardonic wink, "Merde alors, don't you have *enough* to worry about at the moment, M'sieu?"

So Forbes proved they'd been correct in assuming he was a pretty bright guy by nodding and saying, "Right. Let's worry about our outlaws one at a time. That Yank soldier of fortune and, come to think of it, French comrade in arms, have committed no crimes in this particular colony, and as you say, M'sieu *Fontleroy,* we have more important things to worry about. What do you know about French seventy-fives, *Fontleroy*?"

"Me?" asked Gaston innocently. "A banana broker such as myself would know little of such matters, of course. But I have heard France has a new gun we did not, alas, have back in the Franco-Prussian War. It is said to lob a seventy-five-caliber shell a good three kilometers, with some accuracy."

Forbes nodded, and said soberly, "I'm sure an old banana broker like you would know. And the main parts of Zion are nothing like three kilometers south of this bloody river! Do either of you think it's possible they simply showed any old sort of gun to poor Perkins and told him they were seventy-fives? I can't see where on earth they'd have gotten their hands on the real thing, damn it."

Gaston shrugged and replied, "For all a man of the cloth would know, they could have been muzzle-loaders left over from the old Spanish colonial days. But any species of field gun is a thing to consider soberly at this range, hein?"

Forbes agreed, and suggested they get out of their exposed position before someone simply potted off the lot of them with rifle fire. As they all moved along the trail back to town, Forbes asked Captain Gringo what he meant about not showing the note to Olivia Perkins. The American said, "She'll take it bad enough when we have to tell her her husband's dead. Trust me. I know her better than you do, and she has sort of delicate feelings."

"No doubt. But he left specific instructions for her in that last message. Something about a mass and all that rot. I fear I'm not up on Low Church services."

Captain Gringo frowned thoughtfully and took the note out to go over again as he mused aloud, "I don't know whether a Congregationalist is high or low. But I do know Perkins was a *Protestant* minister, and have any of you guys ever heard of a Protestant *mass*?"

Gaston said not to look at him. Dodd didn't say anything. Forbes said he thought they said some sort of mass in the High Anglican Church. But Captain Gringo dug deeper in his Sunday School memories and decided, "Congregationalists are an offshoot of the Calvinist Reformation, and old Calvin was deadset against the Catholic Mass. So, damn, I may have to check this out with Olivia after all. As the widow of a Congregationalist minister, she'd know if Perkins really expected her and her friends—that's us—to go through some sort of rite for him, or if the poor guy was trying to sneak some kind of a *message* to us!"

He handed the note to Dodd and said, "Here, Rev. Read that part about Jeremiah over and tell me what it could mean."

Dodd took the note, but muttered sheepishly, "I used to know the Good Book by heart, of course. But I fear the exact psalm he mentions here is beyond me."

"Swell. You run around conning people about being a man of the cloth, and you don't even have a Bible *on* you, damn it?"

"I'm afraid, *afraid* I say, I left my pocket Bible aboard the ship when they took me off so unexpectedly, Son."

Captain Gringo took the message back and put it away, growling, "There has to be at least one King James edition somewhere in a mission colony established by goddamn lime-juicers. Let's hurry. I have to find one fast."

They did, but as they jogged along Dodd asked why it had to be the King James Version. So Captain Gringo snapped, "You sure must be a great preacher, Dodd. No native Catholic would be familiar with the Protestant King James Version, even if he read English. The Catholic translation of the scriptures into English is worded differently, you chump; and since Perkins was a *real* Protestant minister, he'd have *known* that. He probably knew his King James by heart and tried to slip a coded message past El Chino.

The only trouble is, he did too good a job. How was he to know the rest of us skipped Sunday School all those times?''

Forbes said he had a King James Bible at Government House. So Captain Gringo told Gaston to run ahead and see if they had that sunset gun to work with yet. They split up out front, and he followed Forbes upstairs with Dodd and a couple of constabulary men tagging along. In the governor's office, Forbes began to rummage about in drawers as he kept muttering, "Damn, I know it has to be here somewhere, unless my servants packed it."

"You've already sent some of your stuff home, Sir?"

"Of course, along with my wife and children. She wanted to stay, but our oldest girl's not well and . . . Blast and bloody damn! Why on earth would Matilda have wanted to take my *Bible* along with her?"

Captain Gringo sighed and told him to keep looking. The Reverend D. C. Dodd stood in the way, muttering to himself, and then, just as Captain Gringo was about to tell him to go out in the hall and stay out of the way for God's sake, Dodd snapped his fingers and said, "Jeremiah Eight twenty-two? Of course! Jeremiah, chapter eight, verse twenty-two; and I quote, I say I *quote,* 'Is there no balm in Gilead?' "

The others stared blankly at him. Forbes asked, "I say, that's supposed to be a secret message? It makes no sense!"

But Captain Gringo said, "Not unless you add the refrain, 'Nay, Nay, Never!' Perkins was forced to write that crap about them having artillery. But he managed to sneak in a question: Was there balm, or bombs, or *artillery shells* in Gilead!"

Forbes gasped, "And the answer is nay, nay, never! Or, in other words, to pay no attention to what he'd just written above his closing lines! He *did* go to his maker like a proper Englishman, eh what?"

Captain Gringo tried not to think about the old guy's wife as he nodded soberly amd said, "He was more of a man than a lot of people might have thought. He knew the bluff they intended to pull and he managed to let us know it was a bluff. The cocksuckers got tired of playing stooge for some naughty colonialists and decided to go into business for themselves. But they don't have the weaponry to take us out the easy way!''

Forbes grinned and said, "Then we have nothing to worry about.''

But Captain Gringo shook his head and said, "That's not what I said. El Chino, El Repollo—or whoever's running that gang on the other side of the river—knows he can't hold his gang together if he leads them away empty-handed. So, since he stands to lose most of them in any case if he can't get at that money downstairs, he may just decide that since it's use 'em or lose 'em, he may as well go for broke, the hard way!''

"My God, you're such a cheerful bloke, Captain . . . ah, Crawford. But surely we can stand them off if they simply come at us bare-handed, bandito style!''

"They won't be hitting us bare-handed, Sir. They still have more guns than we do, and we just don't know how many people they have to throw at us in one bunch by the not-so-silvery light of a waning moon.''

He took out his watch to add, morosely, "The moon comes up twenty minutes later every night. That means it ought to be dark as hell right after sundown tonight, and we don't have much time to get set for them.''

"Oh, come now, it's barely noon, and we already have the machine gun you salvaged set up to guard the ford!''

"I know. El Repollo knows it too, thanks to the swell way you kept it under cover while he was over here on this side. The trouble with these Alamo situations, Governor, is that the attacking side has the initiative. That's why Alamos go under so often. With your permission, Sir, I'd like to take that initiative *away* from the sons of bitches!''

"Permission granted," said Governor Forbes soberly. "But just what do you have in mind?''

"I thought I just told you, Sir. As things now stand, they can hit us or not hit us, any time they choose, from any direction. So I guess we'll just have to hit them *first*!''

"Hmm, but you say they have at least three machine

guns to work with, against our one; and that you've no idea how many of them there are or how they're set up?''

Captain Gringo shrugged and said, ''I never said it was going to be *easy*, Governor. I just said it had to be done.''

When he and Dodd got back to the waterfront, Captain Gringo found Gaston and four constabularies hard at work in the hot sun. The sergeant who'd scouted up the work detail was nowhere to be seen. Lots of sergeants were like that. Captain Gringo told Dodd to help the constabularies, took Gaston aside and brought him up to date. Then he said, ''I'm counting on you and the others to hold the river till I get back. If I don't get back, try and hold it anyway.''

''Eh bien, and where will you be while you let me do all the work, as usual, my adventurous youth?''

''Having adventures behind the enemy lines if I can make it by broad-ass daylight. That might not be easy.''

Gaston frowned and said, ''Why go to so much trouble if you are tired of living, Dick? Why not simply take out your shooter of peas and blow your own befuddled brains out? Now that things are coming to a head, the guerrillas will be très alert; and it was hard enough to cross the lines last night in the dark with them half asleep!''

Captain Gringo nodded and said, ''I just said that. Waiting till dark would be waiting too long. If they mean to hit at all, they'll attack early this evening before moonrise. If I can get behind them during this afternoon's siesta and give them something *else* to worry about, you and the others might have less to worry about when the sun goes down.''

He glanced down at his watch and said, ''I don't have all that much time between now and La Siesta. So enough of this bullshit.''

As he turned away, Gaston said, ''Wait, just a little more shit of the bull, Dick! Have you considered that the sad message from Perkins could be shit of the bull as well?''

Captain Gringo frowned and said, "If it's a ruse, it's a pretty complicated one, don't you think?"

"Oui, but the plan of the très sneaky English colonists has been très Byzantine from the beginning. The simple code enclosed with the doleful farewell to a cheating wife would have been even easier to decode if you spent more time in church, and—"

"How did you know Olivia fooled around on the side?" Captain Gringo cut in. So Gaston winked and said, "She comes très noisy. And if *I* discovered this on such short notice, Perkins may have caught her more than once in the past. But never mind how he felt about his wife. Consider the way they insisted on sending the note to her through *you*, knowing you would of course read it and—at the risk of swelling your adorable head—knowing you were slick as the whistle?"

"Jesus, you mean there could be bombs in Gilead after all? I'd better get over there and find out, poco tiempo!"

He legged off down the quay, not bothering to consult the map he'd asked Forbes for as it became obvious Zion was almost a mirror image of the settlement he knew better, north of the river. Zion was larger. There were three church steeples rising above the tin and tile roofing. But here, too, the native barrio began beyond civic improvements, in this case *south* of the main drag. The paved quay gave way to a muddy path along the water's edge, with here and there a rustic landing improvised by the locals. As he'd hoped, he spotted some natives on a wooden dock ahead, repairing nets. A gaily painted little fishing boat was tied up to the landing on the far side. As he joined them, he saw that while the net-menders were of course mestizo, a fair-skinned girl of about twenty with ash-blonde hair was supervising them, seated on a nail keg with her not too long skirts hiked even higher. Assuming she had to be pure Spanish, he addressed her in that language. She answered with a brogue thick enough to cut with a knife, "Ah, lave off the dago blarney and be saying what ye want, me bucko!"

He grinned, took out the survey map he'd picked up and unfolded it as he introduced himself. He handed the map to her, saying, "This chart of the harbor and surrounding area was surveyed years ago when they first made this colony official. I was hoping local fisherfolk would know if all the hurricanes since then have shifted any of the channels enough to matter, Miss . . . ?"

"Fionna O'Shay," she said, adding as she studied the map, "I'd be skipper of *The Irish Rover* ye see there, now that me auld man's under the peat, may he rest in peace, amen. Ye say this is supposed to be a chart of these waters? Faith, ye could never prove it by meself and that's a fact! Few of the inlets and tidal creeks are marked right. The great bay and the Mission River are drawn in right. But it's true the tides, the winds and the mangroves have minds of their own. So the coastlines to the north and south have changed a lot since some sissy Saxon drew this map!"

He started to explain the situation. Halfway through, she told her net-menders they'd done enough and to go seek shade while white people discussed more important matters. As they left, not at all reluctantly, Fionna explained, "Ye can't trust half the black-hearted gazoons, for though I've told them a thousand times, they still take me for English; and they hate the English as much as *I* was raised to!"

She handed the map back to him as she rose from her seat. Her skirts still didn't fall half as far down her bare shins as Queen Victoria might have liked, and Fionna seemed a bit taller and more flat-chested than the current fashions, standing up. He told her, "I want to get well behind the guerrilla lines. Crossing the river in broad daylight would be suicidal, and circling around through the swampy jungle would take longer than I've got. So I was hoping I could recruit native fishermen to run me north, well out to sea of course, and—"

"Say no more," she cut in. "For in God's truth, the fishing business is and will be shot to hell in a hack until this nonsense is ended; and I've nothing better to do this day with me nets all tattered by a fairy shark!"

He shook his head and said, "No offense, Miss Fionna, but I had a more masculine crew in mind. I can't expose a woman to such a risk."

"Jasus, Mary and Joseph, did ye think I led an asey life catching fish for pennies off a lee shore in hurricane waters, ye great fool?"

"No, but—"

"But me no buts, you insulting Yankee, for it's meself or nobody at all at all ye'll go sailing with this morning. I'll vow! Do ye see any other fishing boats in sight? Ye do not. Ye know why? Because any dago with a boat and relations anywhere else along the Mosquito Coast will have loaded his paple and possessions aboard and set sail *days* ago! Me and *The Irish Rover* are still here because the only paple we have on this side of the water lie dead and buried in the shade of Fourteen Holy Martyrs, R.C. That's the staple with the Celtic cross to the left of the great Mormon Temple's staple with no cross at all at all and—"

"Never mind all that," he cut in as he tried to come up with a better idea and couldn't. He said, "I have to get north by sea. But it's only fair to warn you neither you nor your boat might make it back, Fionna."

She shrugged and said, "Aw, Jasus, get in and let's get going, then. De ye always repeat yourself over and over, me bucko?"

By noon Gaston had not only mounted the sunset gun on a limber improvised from a torn-apart ox cart but manhandled it to the outpost guarding the river crossing with the help of Dodd and his reluctant gun crew. Governor Forbes and a detachment of constabulary were already dug in there, looking worried. When Forbes asked if "that other banana broker" had made it, Gaston shrugged and said, "One can only hope so. If anyone can, it shall be Dick. Whether he makes it or not, we shall be up the creek of shit avec no paddle if that droll message from the dying minister was a ruse. There are limits to what even our young friend can do, and if those savages have even one big gun—"

"But Perkins said they were bluffing," Forbes cut in as Gaston just looked disgusted. He turned to Dodd and said,

"Speaking of the shitting of bulls, my mysterious man of the cloth, could you tell me avec no bullshit if you know as much about guns as Dick thinks you do?"

Dodd shrugged modestly and said, "Well, even a man of the cloth who leads an, ah, active life has to know a little about such matters."

"I told you to stop shitting the bull. Do you know how to man a machine gun or don't you?"

"I've fired a Gatling gun in my time. Machine guns are a little new to us old-timers."

"That may be true, but it will have to do. It is not the firing mechanism that is difficult. If you have fired a Gatling, you will know how easy it is to waste ammunition, hosing rapid fire at *air,* hein? Come, I shall show you how to work the action. It is easier in some ways than manning a Gatling. For one thing, one does not have to crank. The important thing with any rapid-fire weapon is to aim it low and at the enemy, not high or between them in a mad display of passion."

Forbes followed them across the trail to where the Maxim had been braced across a log behind a screen of dirt and brush. He asked Gaston, "What about that cannon you just cobbled together?"

Gaston replied, "Merde alors, what about it? I can make a lot of noise with it. We brought all the blank rounds we could find along. But they are simply glorified shotgun shells, mostly pasteboard avec brass bases. I can, when push comes to shove, roar très glorious bursts of harmless smoke and flame at anyone wading at us across that shallow water. It may even give them pause, until they observe nothing seems to be landing in their vicinity. Mais *then* that?"

Forbes said, "I've been thinking about that. Those saluting charges do remind me a lot of shotgun shells. What if we tore open the tops and replaced some of the wadding with, say, rusty nails or even gravel?"

Gaston shrugged and said, "Aside from ruining what is left of the tube, not much. I considered that as soon as I regarded the species of ammunition I had to work with. It seems a lot of bother for little result. It is true small-bore debris fired in one's face by a cannon might smart a bit. But the rifles and machine gun we have here will be throwing *serious* slugs; and if we can not stop them with a platoon of rifles and a machine gun, I fail to see how a handful of pebbles can make much difference. The four-pounder is not a rapid-fire weapon, even firing real ammunition, hein?''

"I wish you wouldn't say things like that."

"I wish I didn't have to. May I ask why you only have thirty constabularies here at the moment, Governor? Surely this can't be your whole police force."

Forbes explained he'd left most of his constabularies in the settlement itself, both to herd the civilians into the swamps to the south if there was no other way to keep them alive at least a few hours more, and to guard the landward approaches should the guerrillas take Captain Gringo's suggestion about a wider circle through the inland jungles. He asked Gaston's views on how much time that would give them, and the Frenchman said, "Perhaps all night. I have been forced to forge my way through lowland jungle, this close to the sea, and found it très tedious. One hopes they may not be that ambitious, or disciplined. The main reason Nicaragua has never seriously disputed these land-grabs of yours along the Mosquito Coast is that even disciplined troops are très difficult to march through such a hell of greenishness. It seems more likely our adorable guerrillas will prefer a more direct approach if they mean to come at all."

Dodd said softly, "They're coming right now, Gents," even as one of the constabularies shouted a challenge. When Forbes saw it was another parley party under a white flag, he shouted to let them come across. So they did.

It was the same El Repollo wearing the same green outfit, and his message hadn't changed much, either. He told Forbes, "El Chino would like for you to know we just shot another Englishman called Webber. We are going to shoot the banker, Riggs, right after La Siesta, if you do not wish for to be reasonable, Señor El Gobernador!''

Forbes gasped and told him that was monstrous as well as out of the question. The guerrilla spokesman shrugged and said, "Hey, is no skin off *my* nariz, one way or the other. I don't care if we shoot them *all*, the stuck-up Anglo pigs."

He winked at Gaston to add, "Hey, I admire your cannon, Frog Face. Didn't it used to stand on a post near the waterfront for to fire blank salutes? You should have repainted it, you poor dumb puller of bluffs!"

Gaston smiled sweetly and said, "There was not time. Thank you for telling us you have spies behind our lines, my little cabbage, and kindly inform your English masters that it fires très explosive shells as well, hein?"

El Repollo frowned and said, "Masters? We don't got no masters, Frog Face. Who told you we got masters, eh?"

"Merde alors, we did not even need the usual little bird. You forget I have *met* your El Chino, *Peon*! If he is your chosen leader, the rest of you may be fit for loading bananas without direct supervision by someone more intelligent. But to rob a blind man without getting caught? Surely you jest! If that unwashed old ruffian is a serious military leader, or even a good pickpocket, I am Queen of the May!"

El Repollo glared and thundered, "Bastards! We shall show you who and what we are! You have my word on that! And you shall swallow your words soon, Frog Face! For because when I come back the next time, I shall shove them down your throat, along with your teeth!"

He turned to splash back across the ford with his standard-bearer. He was so pissed that halfway across, he slipped on the mud and fell on his face in the water. As he rose, dripping wet, to put his soggy green sombrero back on, the constabularies laughed like hell. Forbes had to laugh, too. Then he sobered and told Gaston, "I say, you may have goaded him a bit too far, don't you think?"

Gaston said, "I hope so. I was trying to. If they get mad enough, they may throw caution to the winds and charge us before the sun goes down. If they attack under cover of darkness, I fail to see how we are going to *stop* them, M'sieu!"

• • •

As Fionna O'Shay stood in the stern, poling *The Irish Rover* between the close-set mangroves enclosing the narrow tidal stream that wasn't on any map, Captain Gringo felt completely lost as well. He could see, despite the shady gloom, that the blonde was sweating. But every time he offered to help her pole, she told him to shut his gob. For *The Irish Rover* didn't respond kindly to strange hands trying to direct her bright bluff bows, and there'd be the divvel to pay if she hung her bowsprit up in the mangroves at all at all. He consulted his watch as he asked her just where they might be now, in relation to Gilead. She said, "We're about three miles south of the rail line. Lave it to me, and I'll have ye closer by far by the time this auld passage ends in an inland lagoon I've been after lifting fish from many a time."

"Do you know where that rail line ends, Fionna?"

"I do. It was built by the lumbering paple to avoid a rocky stretch of shallows, about twenty moils up the Mission River. It swings south near the end to a logging camp on the Upper Mission itself. But there'll be nobody there *now* at all at all."

He gasped and moaned, "Oh, Jesus! You mean that train can carry you twenty miles into the jungle in one quick jump, Fionna?"

"It can't carry *us* that far, for it's in *The Irish Rover* we'd be sitting at this moment. But, yes, if ye had the auld railway working, it would get you out to the auld camp in less than an hour. But what of it? The lumber camp's been *abandoned*, Dick."

He said, "Maybe. The bandits had the locomotive running on the tracks yesterday, and I doubt they were just practicing. Have you ever been to this lumber camp?"

"Faith, I've been *everywhere* in this colony, for it was here I was born. Me paple came here from the auld country in the wake of the great potato famine. The Queen had just taken Mission Bay from the Dons, and it was me auld man who thought he'd find more future here, ye see."

She poled on wearily as she added, grim-lipped: "Some future it was, too. Living among the damned auld dagos because all Catholics are despised by the damned auld English! But at laste we never starved, and me auld man doid as the master of his own fishing boat."

She stopped poling a moment to mutter, "Jesus Mary and Joseph, it's hot, even in the shade, at this toim of the dayo." Then she slipped her sweaty blouse off over her head, dropped it and picked up the pole again to go on, naked from the waist up.

He was too polite to stare. But he couldn't help noticing she wasn't as flat-chested as he'd assumed. Her small, firm breasts looked like cupcakes glazed with sweat as she poled on with her strong young torso swaying gracefully and teasingly in the dappled shade. He took out his .38 and fieldstripped it on the thwart between them. It didn't need cleaning, but a guy had to keep his eyes *somewhere* without being obvious. Fionna asked, "Why did ye bring only one wee pistol along if we're on serious business, Dick?"

He said, "It's serious enough. But I sneak better with my weapon tucked under one shoulder. One rifle, or even a machine gun, wouldn't be much use to me in a head-on gunfight with a whole guerrilla band."

"Anyone could have told ye that. So why would you be after sneaking in behind them at all at all?"

"I'm not sure yet. It depends on what I find when I get there. Let's get back to that lumber camp. What do you remember about it?"

She shrugged as she poled, moving her sweet little tits in a most provocative way, and said, "Och, it was just a great clearing in the woods, with a few shacks for the workers, a stame-powered sawmill and a winch to haul timber from the river because they couldn't raft it all the way to the coast with them shallows in the wayo. They'd had some Indian thrubbles in the early days, or at least they'd seen Indians lurking about and *thought* they meant thrubble. Ye know how the English are. But the great gun they brought in was never used; and the last toim I saw it, it had gone all green with the rains."

"Oh my God! Are you saying there's a *cannon* or, worse yet, *was* a cannon at that lumber camp?"

"Och, it was auld and rusty and not a great gun besides. It was only one of thim muzzle-loaders lift over from the auld days. They couldn't have paid much for the wee thing. Ye know how cheap the English are, Dick. What's the matter? Ye look like ye've just heard the banshee, and there's not even an *Indian* in this darling swamp!"

He said, "I may have heard the banshee just now, at that, if we're talking about premonitions of death and disaster! I may owe another ghost an apology if the mastermind behind all this is even more Machiavellian than even my pal Gaston thought!"

He'd naturally filled Fionna in on the whole story as they sailed up the coast together, so she nodded and said, "Och, no Frenchman or even an Irishman can come close to being as treacherous as the English, for don't they beat us every time, no matter how cleverly we plot? You'd be thinking ye were meant to read that coded message so they'd be after taking ye by surprise when they fired on yez with a big gun. Then, since ye'd been led to expect no big gun at all at all, ye'd think, when yez saw ye'd been tricked, that what was coming at yez was thim real modern weapons instead of just one auld brass muzzle-loader, right?"

He grinned up at her and said, "I thought you Irish weren't as good at plotting treachery. That's pretty complicated, but it sure figures to *work* if my pals at the ford buy it. On the other hand, old Perkins may have simply been told to write that they had those seventy-fives, and since he hadn't seen any, he tried to tell us it was a bluff. How the hell would a prisoner know about a gun they never showed him? I'll know better, later, If we never see the minister alive again, we'll know he was a hero. If he's still alive, he has to be a rat. How far are we from that lagoon now?"

"We're there," grunted Fionna, poling them between close-set mangrove roots with a last mighty effort to pop *The Irish Rover* out into a sunlit patch of open water. She looked even more naked now. But that wasn't why he'd recruited her. So he looked the other way as she poled them across the little lagoon and grounded the bows against a muddy patch between two big buttress-rooted trees. As he spotted the path leading off through the jungle from there, Fionna said, "That gum-cruiser's trail will be after lading you to the outskirts of Gilead, Dick. How long will I be after waiting for you here?"

He leapt ashore before he turned with a smile and said, "You've done more than enough; and if I make it I'm going to ask the governor to hang a medal on you, English or not. But you'd better not stick around. You'd better pole back to sea and sail south to safety, Doll."

She leapt ashore after him, and might have fallen had not he grabbed her to steady her when one foot slipped in the mud. He grabbed her the best way he could without taking time to think, and that one little tit felt better than it looked before he hastily let go. Fionna took his hand and put it back where it had been as she said, "Before ye go, would ye take lave of a lady like a gintleman?"

He gulped and said, "I'd love to if there was time, Fionna."

"Och, how much toim does it take to kiss a gorl, ye great fool?"

He laughed and said, "Oh well, since you put it *that* way," and reeled her in for a friendly wet smack. It might not have been so wet had Fionna kept her tongue in her mouth. When they came up for air, she was blushing and he was stiff as a poker inside his pants. But she said, "There, now I'm satisfied. Or at least I'll be letting ye go for now. When ye get done doing whatever it is ye'll be after doing, it's here I'll be waiting for ye, Dick."

"Fionna, it's not safe. I may be able to work back to our lines another way, and that's where I want to find you when I do, see?"

"I do not. Ye said on the way there was only one crossing and that that was where the serious foiting would be taking place, ye great fool!"

"Yeah, but—"

"Och, but me no buts and be off with ye. For the sooner ye get going, the sooner ye'll be after getting back; and it's another grand kiss ye'll owe me when ye foind me here to welcome ye back aboard!''

He didn't have time to argue, so he didn't take it. He kissed her again and took off through the trees. As the shade grew darker, he got out his .38. Fionna had assured him nobody was gathering gum these days. But a path was always a great place for an ambush, even though he had to follow it in country he didn't know.

He was glad he had, after the trail had snaked him past a couple of swamps and a broad patch of what might have looked like open mossy ground if a saltwater crocodile's eyes and nostrils hadn't been showing above the green surface scum. A quarter-mile on, the path widened to become a wagon trace leading into what had to be the outskirts of town—unless someone had built scattered shacks among the second-growth sapling all around just for the hell of it. He slowed down, gun in hand, all too aware as he moved on that although it was siesta time in a ghost town, he could still be making a big mistake!

It got easier as he worked into the more built-up parts of the barrio because now he could sneak along lanes and alleyways with solid and, he hoped, empty housing to either side. Somewhere in the distance a guitar was strumming a lazy tune. So he moved faster. People hardly ever played guitars on patrol, or even on guard, if they were serious. He knew nobody would be expecting an attack from the north, if an attack was what he was up to, exactly. So far, he was simply playing it by ear until he could figure some way to create a diversion on this side of the river.

He peered around an alley corner to spot the rail yards he and Gaston had found earlier. The same locomotive stood in the same spot, its boiler cold. He grimaced and said to himself, "Right. It *was* the old brass cannon they were after! If they planned a flank attack, there'd be smoke out that Shay's funnel right now. It takes hours to get up steam from scratch with green firewood. So they can't be planning an end run by rail. Let's not worry whether they're too stupid to think of that or too smart to march the twenty miles back on the far side of the river the hard way!''

It would have been risky to cross the open yards. So he worked his way around them through the close-packed little native shacks. He heard no signs of life from any of them. Why should a brave soldado and his adelita take over a squalid shack when there were nicer empty houses to the south across the tracks?

It took him more time than he had to waste, but at last he was south of the tracks in yet another alley. He climbed up on a fence to see if he could get his bearings again. It was easy. The bell tower of the schoolhouse he remembered rose well above the lower roofing between. That bigger tin roof a little closer had to be the warehouse Estralita had led him and Gaston to. He considered making for that first. He decided it wasn't worth it. He had plenty of waterproof matches; but even if he burned their supplies, it would take them too long to get hungry, now that their adelitas had had time to lug at least enough food for the next few meals to their own scattered shack-ups. The guns and ammo he and Gaston had seen there as well was no doubt even more well distributed, so what the hell.

He worked his way to the vicinity of the schoolhouse and then had to circle wide to avoid the open schoolyard, taking up even more precious time. As he hunkered in the last cover between him and the blank back wall of the schoolhouse, he consulted his watch and swore under his breath. Where in the hell was all the time going today? Why was it that an hour felt so much longer to a man in a dentist's chair than it did to a man on a porch swing with a pretty girl? He cursed himself now for having taken time to kiss Fionna *twice*. He had to do something while the siesta kept the surrounding streets reasonably clear, and so far hadn't even *thought* of anything!

He eased out of the alley entrance, glanced up and down the cinder-covered lane between him and the back of the school and dashed across to dive into the weeds at the base of the blank wall and roll under the building. The crawl space was about four feet between the bare dirt under the

school and the overhead wooden flooring. It was less
where the big timber joists held the flooring up. The main
timbers all around him were solid mahogany. It figured.
mahogany was one of the few woods that didn't rot fast in
this climate, and it cost a lot less where it grew.

He heard voices, and crawled that way until he was right
under the room they were coming from. Someone topside
was having a hell of an argument, and a couple of the
voices were speaking with English accents as well as in
that language. So there went a fib that El Repollo had been
trying to sell!

Someone was insisting in English, "Goddamn it, El
Chino. You know we never meant it to go this far! There
was nothing in the original plan about actually harming
anyone! If we let you shell Zion, English women and
children could be killed!"

El Chino answered, "Si, but not too many, Señor
Webber. I feel sure your stubborn gobernador will give us
the money before too many of his people land about him in
bits and pieces, eh?"

Another English voice said, "You don't know Governor
Forbes as well as *we* do, then! He simple *can't* turn over
funds left under the protection of the Crown! He and all
his men will go down fighting first!"

A voice Captain Gringo recognized as that of El Repollo
said, "Bueno. After we kill all the bastards, we shall
simply open the vaults ourselves, eh?"

Webber protested, "My God, that could mean the deaths
of hundreds of innocent people, including some of your
own race! Can't you see that, El Repollo?"

"Shit, Hombre, nobody who runs away from me is a
brother or sister of me and mine! We ain't bad guys. We
asked them polite. But if they wish for to fight us for the
money, it is not our fault if a few baby bottles get broken,
is it?"

"Be reasonable, Gentlemen! This isn't the deal we
made at all! Didn't we pay you enough already, El Chino?
Didn't we get you all those supplies and all those nice new
guns?"

El Repollo said, "Hey, don't talk to *him*. Talk to *me*!

You think you *own* us because you give us a few presents and a little dinero, you cheap bastards? They got *millions* over there in Zion. You expect us to let them keep it when we got all the guns we need for to take it away from them? Santa Maria, do we look like men or chickens?''

Another English voice moaned, ''Damn you, Webber! I was against this mad scheme from the beginning! I warned you we might not be able to control these perishing vagabonds!''

Webber, whoever he was, said, ''Shut up. I haven't lost control. One simply has to know how to deal with natives.'' Then he said, ''We've argued about it enough, you lot. We forbid you to fire into Zion, and that's that. In case you've forgotten, I'd best remind you just who's in *command* here!''

He probably should have worded it another way, although the results might have been the same. El Repollo didn't even answer. He, or somebody, simply started throwing lead, lots of lead!

As guns roared above him, Captain Gringo was rolling away before the first body thudded to the floor. But a couple of wild shots sent slugs and slivers down into the dirt where he'd just been, anyway. By the time he was clear enough to pause and listen again, it had gotten quiet, save for the drip-dropping of blood through the bullet holes in the flooring. He heard El Chino ask mildly, ''For why did you shoot all those people, my boy?''

El Repollo replied, ''For because I was tired of listening to them, Grandfather. What is the difference? I told the other English we were going to shoot them, anyway. So now I do not have any fibs on my conscience, see?''

''But my Grandson, they promised for to give us more money before we left, no?''

''Si, but I spit on the pennies they meant to give us, and now that they are out of the way, we can get down to business and make some *real* money! I go now for to see about moving that cannon into place for tonight. Are you coming with me?''

''You go ahead. I shall get someone to clean up this

mess you just made in my nice office. But did you not say *they* have a cannon, too?''

"Si, but our own shoots cannonballs and grape. Theirs is just a toy for shooting blanks. Stay here if you wish. Do not go out in the hot sun. I will send someone to tidy up from one of the occupied buildings all around.''

Captain Gringo listened soberly as El Repollo clumped off just above him. *Now* was a hell of a time to find out those buildings he'd slipped between across the street were filled with guerrillas! He knew he'd never luck past them again, after all that gunplay, even if it *was* siesta time!

He couldn't do anything about the situation above his head right now, either, without at least a few sticks of dynamite. Firing blind up through the floor would just give his position away; and how many thugs could he hope to even wing with six lousy shots and one hell of a lot of luck? He started crawling the other way. If he had more dry splinters to work with, he could maybe set the place on fire, he supposed, but so what? They'd just step outside, and it wasn't such a hot idea to set a house he was hiding under on fire, in any case.

He crawled to the far side and peered out to mutter, "Nuts." There was a weedy patch of abandoned garden, offering crawling cover to a picket fence he could probably punch through. But not if the house beyond was full of guerrillas. He had to just lay low until things calmed down again, even though time was running out and he didn't even dare *smoke*!

He put his .38 away. It wasn't doing anything out, but getting dirty in any case. Outside he could see legs moving up and down around the school. Above, feet were thumping on the floorboards and things were being dragged across them. He looked at his watch: it was pushing three, goddamn its nervous hands, and they might not settle down outside again at all for the rest of the afternoon. He was probably safe where he was, and it would be easy enough to sneak out after sundown. But he goddamn-it didn't *have* that much time! He knew as well as if El Repollo had just told him personally that they'd be opening up with that muzzle-loader just after sundown—and the others weren't expecting artillery fire at all!

A pair of shapely female legs moved along the side of the school until he had a better view of them than he really wanted, trim as her ankles might be. What the hell was some dame doing there? She was standing out of sight of the school entrance and yard, he could see. If it had been a man, he'd have worried about him taking a leak right in his face. But that couldn't be what a *dame* had in mind, could it?

It wasn't. Estralita suddenly dropped to all fours and whipped under the schoolhouse as if to join him. But, from the way she gasped when she spotted him—and might have screamed if he hadn't clapped a palm across her mouth and rolled her onto her back—she was more surprised than he was. He growled, "I have a gun. Do you think I might have to use it?"

She stared wide-eyed up at him and tried to shake her head. He removed his hand from her mouth but left it on her chest, just in case. It seemed no matter how casually a guy put his hand to a bare-chested female these days, he wound up with a handful of tit. Hers were a lot bigger and softer than Fionna's, but not at all bad.

He whispered, "Bueno. I'll tell you what I'm doing under the house if you'll tell me, Estralita. You go first."

She sighed and said, "It is too hot for to work; and even if it was not, I do not like the sight of blood. El Chino has everyone cleaning the floors upstairs, and I did not think they would miss me if I slipped away."

"Let's hope not! Are all those Englishmen dead?"

"Si, I do not know for why. I came when I heard gunshots. My curiosity is always getting me in trouble. When I saw work was involved, I decided I had seen enough. Are you going to kill me?"

"Now why would I want to do that, Estralita?"

"They say you are muy malo, Captain Gringo. Some say you are even meaner than El Repollo, and he is so mean the Devil fears for his soul around him! But do not kill me, por favor! I would much rather be your adelita than a corpse!"

He noticed she'd moved one dainty hand up to help him massage her naked breast as she guided his wrist. He said, "I thought you already *had* a soldado. Aren't you the adelita of El Chino?"

She sighed and said, "Si, alas. He chose me because I am the most beautiful woman in the band. But I had nothing to say about the matter, and in God's truth, had it been up to me, I would have chosen someone younger and better-looking, like *you!*"

"Don't you really love El Chino?"

"How could I know? He has never even touched me when we are alone. As you know, he feels me up all the time when other men are watching, for to look like a real hombre himself, I think. It feels good to be felt up. But, alas, he never even does *that* enough for to satisfy me! Would you like to feel me up, por favor?"

He grinned down at her and said, "May as well. We don't have any books to read down here while we wait."

He meant to kind of keep her distracted as they let things sort of settle down outside. Even if she hadn't been passed around among the guerrillas—at least recently—the big, sluttish brunette was so stupid she seemed a bit repellent to a man of his tastes. But as he ran his free hand down her lush curves—taking his time, since he was in no hurry—she somehow started looking better by the minute; and by the time she'd lifted her skirts out of the way and guided his hand into her damp black welcoming mat, she looked so pretty he was tempted to kiss her. So he did, if only to keep her quiet, of course, as she moaned in pleasure with her turgid clit throbbing between his questing fingers. She kissed with her tongue like Fionna, and though it didn't feel at all the same, it felt great and served to remind him of the erection he'd left Fionna with, unsatisfied.

So though he knew he'd hate himself in the morning, and that Fionna would be mad as hell if she ever found out, it seemed silly to say no when Estralita pleaded "Oh, do not *tease* me, Querido! *Do* it! I want to come right, with a real man, after all this time!"

Besides, he thought, as he tore his pants open and rolled on top of her, how the hell was Fionna ever going to find out? *He* sure wasn't ever going to tell her, even if he got out of this mess alive!

So the mess he was in proceeded to screw hell out of him; and though her brains didn't seem to improve with passion, he saw she was at least smart enough to bite her lush lower lip and come silently with her eyes closed while he pounded her to glory.

Naturally, once wasn't enough for the hard-up pretty moron. So, since he couldn't go anywhere else anyway right now, they stripped all the way and he went back in her, stark, atop their spread-out clothing. They still wound up with lots of red dust on his knees and in her hair as they made barnyard love under the schoolhouse in the dirt. He wasn't going to look any sillier, or wind up any deader, if anyone caught him laying the official leader's adelita, so what the hell.

After he'd come in her a couple of times, he began to wonder why. But Estralita stared up adoringly at him and murmured, "Oh, I am so happy, you wicked muchacho. You certainly know how to make a woman feel like a woman. May we do it some more, Querido?"

He shook his head and said, "Hold the thought. We're not safe here. Do you think you could help me sneak out of here, Estralita?"

"Of course. Everyone has to do as I say except the officers. But where do you wish for to take me for to fuck some more?"

That wasn't exactly the way he'd have put it. But he said, "I'd like to get over to that warehouse again. I know the way from there."

"You speak of *food* at a time like this?"

"Take it easy. We could be *alone* in there, on top of nice soft sacking, see?"

"Oh, bueno, this dirt under me feels most hard with a man your size on top of me. Let me up. I think it is safe for to duck out now."

She was right. They quickly dressed, and he let her go first to make sure the coast was clear. They were a lot less likely to shoot her on sight. She waved him out, and they walked innocently away to duck into the first alley they could get to. Then she led him through the maze to the corrugated metal warehouse. As they got inside she slid the door shut, saying, "It locks from the inside. So we are free for to have more fun. Any adelita who comes looking for more provisions will just think we are closed for now, eh?"

He said, "Great. But un momento, Querida. I have to do something outside, first, see?"

"Use that little side door. What is it you wish for to do? Oh, never mind. Sometimes it makes *me* want to piss afterwards, too."

He kissed her gallantly and told her to wait for him in the back. Then he moved to the side exit, made sure it was safe and stepped out.

He made the alley-dash for the rail yards fast, knowing she'd be a yeller if she got suspicious. He climbed up into the unguarded Shay locomotive, checked the water gauges, and when he saw the boiler was filled, popped the firebox open. Someone had been kind enough to leave newspaper and kindling on hand. He tossed it in and lit it, using all the kindling, since he was only going to get to do this once. Then, as the interior of the firebox lit up with flames, he started chunking the driest logwood he could find into the tender built into the back of the Shay. While he waited to see if he'd wind up with more smoke or fire, he got to work on the throttle and safety valve. As always, a coil of bailing wire was hooked to an inside wall of the cab for emergency repairs. Wiring the safety valve shut was hardly what one might call a repair. But he didn't intend to ride the locomotive anywhere. He checked the firebox again. Things were looking up. Thanks to a couple of days in the hot sun, the wood, though green-cut, was drier this afternoon, and a lot of what hadn't dried out was sun-baked pitch. He used a poker to move the first wood all the way back, then stuffed the firebox as full as it would go with more wood. As he slammed the door shut, the steam gauge was already starting to tremble. It was still going to take at least an hour, but at least he had something more interesting than Estralita's ass heating up now.

He leaped down and legged it back to the warehouse in

hopes she hadn't had time to get suspicious. When he saw the front door gaping wide, he saw she had—and they said hell had no fury like a dumb Spanish spitfire scorned.

He grinned crookedly and muttered, "Shit, I wasn't gone *that* long." Then he dashed to the rear of the warehouse to see if by any chance anyone *else* around here had been acting dumb.

They had. Two of the machine guns he'd seen back there before were long gone. But one still lay in its unopened crate. El Chino could only have so many machine-gunners, after all.

He ripped the crate open. The Maxim was covered with a thick coating of grease. Tough shit. This was neither the time to worry about clean clothes or cleaning guns. He found another crate of ammunition, and, better yet, it was machine-gun ammo, already belted!

He wrapped a half-dozen belts around his body, over the shoulder and riding on one hip. Then he started clipping other belts together end-to-end. He'd managed to form one long belt, but still had more to go when he heard shouting voices coming his way. So he hauled the Maxim out of its crate, armed it with one end of the longer belt and started backing for the side entrance with the Maxim on his hip and the ammo belt following them across the floor like a pull toy. He almost made it. Then a quartet of sombreroed guerrillas dashed in the front doorway, waving guns and saying dreadful things about Yanqui spies. So, hoping the greasy, untested Maxim wouldn't blow up in his hands, Captain Gringo pulled the trigger and mowed all four of them down as he backed out the other door!

As he headed for the nearest alley entrance, a bullet whipped over his head. He fired a burst into the gun smoke he spotted up at the next corner and kept going without waiting to see the results.

He saw yet more sombreros blocking his way at the far end of the alley and threw curses and a burst of hot lead at them as he realized they knew this maze better than he did. There had to be a better way out of it. The way he chose was crude but effective. The shanties of the barrio were built cheap and flimsy. Captain Gringo wasn't. So he simply bulled his way through the back wall of the nearest shack.

He'd expected it to be empty. But an ugly adelita had been frying refritos when the shooting started and was still hunkered down by her camp stove when Captain Gringo exploded through the thin plank wall at her in a cloud of splinters, covered with grease and black with gun smoke, the big gun on his hip and long ammo belt lashing behind him like a dragon's tail! She shouted, "Ay, El Diablo!" and tore out the front as Captain Gringo tripped over the cook stove and kicked it into a corner with a curse. He knew what could happen if he followed a screaming woman out *that* way. So he went *another* way, through yet another wall, as bullets started popping through the front wall and the side wall caught on fire, thanks to the spilled stove!

To call the next forty-five minutes or so a confusing, running gunfight would be gross understatement. The enraged if confused guerrillas had the advantage of numbers and *thought* they knew every way out of the area. Captain Gringo had the advantage of automatic fire, desperation and the knowledge that since he didn't know anyone he liked in this part of the barrio, he was free to fire at any hint of movement or set fire to anything he passed that looked inflammable.

So that's what he started doing. The first shack he'd sent up in flames after semi-demolishing it had been an accident, but it seemed a swell way to add to the confusion and, better yet, to keep anyone from wondering about the wood smoke rising from the rail yards somewhere around here. It was easy enough. All he had to do after kicking through a mess of sun-baked siding was put a match to the nice dry splinters and push on as the shack filled with smoke. It beat moving through the streets and alleyways and wasn't a whole lot slower. From time to time he had to dart across a yard or a street at the end of a block, and almost every time he did the results were noisy as hell. But a guy popping through a blank wall firing a hot machine gun at you from the hip tended to unsettle even a well-thought-out ambush, and those guerrillas who didn't die on the spot tended to stop thinking and just start *running*!

But Captain Gringo knew, as he crouched in the ruins of a deserted shack to thread one of his remaining ammo belts into the smoldering action of the once-too-greasy and now sort of fried machine gun, that he was running out of time as well as low on ammunition. He could have beelined out of the barrio in less than five minutes. But every time he tried that, he seemed to run into guys with other ideas and had to crab sideways spitting lead. He was sort of turned around, after all those side trips through walls and fences. But he could still tell north from south by the slanting rays of the late afternoon sun. So he decided he'd just better blast his way out to the north and the hell with it, as soon as he got his breath back.

A few miles away near the river crossing, El Repollo stood by the old brass cannon almost as green as his hat and demanded "Well?" as the runner he'd sent staggered back to him. The runner gasped, "El Chino says to get back to him with these other men, poco tiempo! All hell has broken loose around our headquarters. Shacks are going up in smoke, and some maniac is smoking up the whole place with a machine gun! Estralita says she has reason to believe it could be that Captain Gringo, and El Chino says he needs help no matter *who* it might be!"

El Repollo shook his head and said, "Run back and tell them to just do the best they can for now. It is most obviously just an attempt at diversion. The real fight is here at the river, and we are ready for to start it. Go, muchacho! Tell my grandfather, if he can't stand a little noise to just bring the others out this way and let the barrio burn. Who cares if an empty town burns, eh?"

As the runner took off, the green-hatted leader turned to his reluctant gun crew and said, "Bueno. Let us give them a round or two as we wait for sunset, eh?"

Someone objected, "But El Repollo, I thought we did not intend to charge across the shallows before dark."

"Do as I say, goddamn your mother's milk! It will be

dark soon enough, and it takes a lot of cannonballs for to soften up even a weak position!''

So they got to it and lobbed the first round of solid shot to the south, over the treetops and across the river. It fell a bit short, but not short enough to cheer Captain Gringo's comrades guarding the ford. As the heavy cast-iron ball hit just at the water's edge and spattered everyone nearby with mud and water, Forbes moaned, "Oh, no! They *do* have artillery after all!"

From his own position behind the sunset gun, Gaston called out, "Eh bien, hold your positions, everyone. That was solid shot, not a shell!''

A nearby nervous constabulary grunted, "Coo, what's the difference, if you're under it when it hits! They have the flaming *range* on us, Frenchy! We have no bloody targets for our rifles, and they have us targeted indeed!''

Another ball screamed over to smash into a tree behind them and send it crashing as Forbes ran over to Gaston and said, "They have us bracketed, goddamn it! What are we to do?''

"Hold our positions, of course. I tried to tell people this at Sedan, but would they listen? Mais non, they fell back, just as the Boche hoped they would, and when Bismarck's infantry charged, there was nothing for even a hero like myself to do but run like a deer! I make it one muzzle-loader, black powder and solid shot. So how much damage can they do, and, regard, I keep hearing small-arms fire in the distance when the wind is right. So our friend Dick is up to something interesting, *too*! Let us not get the wind up until we have to, hein?''

But, just as he finished, a third big cast-iron ball screamed down out of the blue to land right on D. C. Dodd's machine-gun position to crush the rear action of the Maxim and leave Dodd a screaming mess writhing away from it, trailing blood and guts!

He was silent and, mercifully, dead by the time Forbes and some others reached him. Gaston didn't leave his post by the sunset gun. He'd been under fire before. He yelled, "Merde alors! Everyone hold his triple-titted place! Can't you see this harassing fire is *intended* to make you run about like headless chickens?''

One of the gun crew he'd dragooned into helping him sobbed, ''I'd rather be a bloody chicken with a head than without one! If it's all the same to the rest of you, I'm off!''

Gaston drew his .38 and said, ''No, you're not. I love you all like my own children, but I'll shoot the first species of yellow dog who misbehaves before the enemy.''

''Frenchy, it's no bloody use! We've lost our only real weapon, and at this rate they won't even have our flaming rifles to worry about by the time they're ready to charge!''

There was a murmur of agreement from the others around the big but useless gun. Another cannonball slammed down; and though this one didn't take anyone out, a constabulary gasped, as it made the earth tremble under them, ''See what he means, you dumb little frog?''

Gaston stared morosely across the river. A haze of white smoke drifted above the treetops over that way, a little to the left of where Gaston had ranged on the sound of the enemy gun. He nodded and said, ''Allowing for the trade winds, the couchon is about where my old ears said.''

Someone else said, ''So what? There's nothing we can *do* about it!''

Gaston sighed, picked up one of the grotesque rounds he'd cobbled together that afternoon while they waited and shoved it into the breech of the crudely mounted four-pounder, saying, ''Eh bien, the rest of you move off, très far, and hit the adorable deck. I do not think this is going to work. But you are right. We have to do *something* before we are swatted like flies in any case, hein?''

Then he closed his eyes and pulled the laynard.

The sunset gun didn't blow up in his face, after all. A few seconds after it roared on their side of the river, they heard another roar among the trees across the way. Gaston blinked in surprise and said, ''Sacre goddamn! I am a genius instead of a suicidal maniac, after all! Let us give them more of the same, hein?''

They did. What Gaston had doped out was crude as hell

but still more effective than solid shot. Having plenty of blank rounds but no shells to work with, Gaston had begun by cutting apart some extra—mostly cardboard—rounds with his knife. Removing the brass base of a round allowed it to fit in the barrel like a shell to begin with. But since even a big wad of cardboard wasn't likely to travel far or do anything important when it got there, he'd cannibalized more wadding from other blanks to seal the open ends left by the removal of the bases; and as long as he had them open anyway, tossed a handful of gravel into the loose powder for luck. The nitrate-impregnated wadding was meant to burn well to avoid clogging the tube of even a sunset gun, so he used a lot, knowing it would act as a quick fuse when the propellant charge blew it out the far end . . . he hoped. By taping one of his glorified firecrackers to more businesslike regular blanks, Gaston had devised rounds that would either act as old-fashioned shells of the Napoleonic era or, if all the powder went off at once inside the gun, split the tube and kill him instead. So Gaston was relieved as well as pleased to discover his invention really worked. He'd had no intention of even trying it unless there was no other hope. But now that he had, he made up for lost time by lobbing round after round in El Repollo's general direction.

Most of it landed nowhere near the enemy's own crude artillery position, of course. Even if Gaston had known exactly where to aim, the clumsy cardboard bombs, unaffected by the rifling of the sunset gun, sailed ass over teakettle in high arcs to poop out due to wind resistance and simply spin down without any great velocity. But, as most detonated as air bursts before landing, the results were frightening as hell. A couple of guerrilla gunners were already running as El Repollo snarled, ''Goddamn it, stand like men and help me! They don't have our range! They're just firing wild, see?''

Then a lucky round came down closer, not on El Repollo directly, but into the open ammunition cart a few yards from him and his brass cannon. That wasn't far enough for safety when the whole mess went off with a thunderous roar—ending El Repollo's violent career in a manner more merciful, if messy, than he deserved!

On the far side of the river Gaston heard the roar, blinked and muttered, "Sacre bleu, how did I *do* that?"

Then, from a greater distance—but not far enough for his eardrums' comfort—Gaston heard an even more thunderous explosion and said, "Now I *know* I didn't do *that*!"

He hadn't. It was even rougher on Captain Gringo's eardrums when the locomotive boiler he'd left on the stove with its safety valve wired shut finally built up enough steam pressure to overcome its very solidly riveted seams and explode in a huge ball of scalding steam and flying boiler plate! The shock wave alone flattened everything within blocks, including the schoolhouse with El Chino and Estralita inside it.

El Chino's left leg had been amputated at the knee by a hot slab of boiler plate slicing through the tin roof, and he lay screaming like a stuck pig in the wreckage. But the tough Estralita had gotten off with no more than cuts and bruises. So she was able to shove the door that had pinned her to the floor off her, stagger to her feet and start groping her way out of the wreckage as the old man screamed, "Querida! Help me! I am badly hurt! I can not get out, and this wreckage seems to be on fire!"

Estralita looked back, saw the blue smoke curling up here and there where the demolition had buried stoves and lamps under shattered planking and said, "Si, the whole place is about to burn, Old Man. So this muchacha shall say adios before she gets her hair singed! The game is up. You were crazy to take on the British Empire in the first place!"

"Goddamn your cruel heart, come back here and *help* me!" sobbed El Chino, even as he saw Estralita had no such intentions. She was having enough trouble crawling out of the smashed timbers and kindling wood the building had been reduced to. El Chino snarled in mixed pain and rage, drew his .45 and yelled, "Come back, you puta!"

Then, as he saw she was still crawling away from him, he fired. The bullet took Estralita right between the cheeks of her voluptuous rump, went up her ass and didn't stop going until it hit bone above her heart. El Chino grunted with as much satisfaction as a man about to either bleed or burn to death could feel; then he put another round into the big brunette's dead flesh. And then, as he saw the wood near him burst into rapidly growing flames, El Chino shrugged fatalistically, put the smoking muzzle of the .45 into his own mouth and pulled the trigger.

Nothing happened. El Chino pulled the trigger again and again even as he realized, sickly, that the last round he'd wasted in the dead girl was the last in his revolver!

He had other bullets in his gun belt, if only he could get *at* them in time. But he was buried chest-deep in debris, weak from the loss of blood as well as from his age, and he knew now how he was about to die.

Off to the north, where Fionna O'Shay and *The Irish Rover* waited, the distant detonations had been taken for a thunder squall by the wiry blonde, even though the sky above looked too clear for thunder to her experienced fisherwoman's eye.

She shrugged and went on pan-frying the mangrove snapper she'd caught in the lagoon to occupy her time while she waited. A ''dacent Irish gorl'' had trouble making friends in a world where most of the unattached males she met were either a bit dark for her liking or, worse yet, English. She wondered, as she squatted by her little fire near the beached bow of her boat, whether Darling Dick was at least a Deathbed Catholic. But she'd already decided never to ask him. What a girl didn't know couldn't be held against her by the saints, and Jesus Mary and Joseph, he was such a grand handsome devil and what could be after *keeping* him all this time?

She'd combed her hair and put her blouse back on again as she cooked the fish, knowing it would be ready for him by sunset and that he'd be back by then if he came back at all. So she felt she had the right to display some dis-approval when Captain Gringo suddenly staggered out of the jungle at her covered with grease, soot and splinters.

She said, ''Mary, Mother of God, is that any way to come to the table? It's a foin mess ye've made of your clothes, and the rest of ye looks as if ye'd been shoveling coal in a windstorm! But I've a bar of naphtha soap in the boat, and by the toim ye get cleaned up this fish will be ready."

He sank to his knees beside her and said, "No time for either. I think I discouraged anyone from trying to follow me further by the time I used up the whole works, but . . ."

"Whole works of what, Dick?" she asked, still moving the pan to keep the fish from sticking.

He shook his head wearily and said, "I swiped a machine gun back there and blew a lot of guys away before it finally warped too badly to fire any more, and I had to just drop it and start running. It feels like I've run a hundred miles. But I'm getting my breath back now. So get in the boat and I'll shove us off, see?"

"Faith, I see nothing of the kind. For this fish is fair on its way to being done and the auld tide's out even if I meant to sail by sunset, hungry, with such a dorty man! Go get that soap and make yourself dacent in the lagoon. I won't look, if that's what you're worried about. But get *to* it, man, for it's like a fish you smell yourself right now. How in the divvel did ye manage to run into *fish* in yon town of Gilead? Och, of course, it was dried cod someone had lying about. There's no mistaking the smell of codfish."

He moved quickly away, climbed into *The Irish Rover* and found the laundry soap under the rear thwart among other such supplies. He knew this was crazy. But if they couldn't put out through the mangroves until the tide rose again, at least he could go down clean as well as fighting if he hadn't thrown that last bunch off.

He put his boots, gun and wallet on a thwart and went over the side, clothes and all, to undress in the shallow water with the hull between him and Fionna. He'd *noticed* Estralita seemed a little sweaty under the schoolhouse, way back when. But he'd been sweaty and dirty as well, so what was a little codfish among friends?

He soaped all the parts of him that Estralita had stunk up with extra care and let them soak as he ran lots of soap over his wet clothing. Most of the gun grease was on his pants. Most of the fishy body odor of Estralita was, too, of course. So he spent more time on the pants with the grease-cutting naphtha soap, and had it about whipped by the time Fionna called, "What's after keeping you, Dick? The fish is ready and it will soon be dark. Put on your damned auld wet pants if you're bashful, and come taste what I have for ye here!"

He laughed, even though he wasn't sure she could have meant that the way it could be taken. He draped most of his clothes over the edge of the boat. Then he picked up the .38 and moved around to join her, wearing nothing but his soggy shorts. As he hunkered down across the fire from her, Fionna shot a thoughtful glance at the white cotton bulge between his muscular thighs and said, "Well, if it's a *chill* ye'd be wanting down there, it's not *me* that will be feeling it."

"You wanna bet?"

"Och, be off with the blarney, ye fool. It's not aven dark yet, and we've until the tide comes back in around eleven to discuss romance. Eat and get some strength back."

He did. He hadn't known how hungry he'd gotten till he dug into the tasty plump snapper. Fionna's tea was pretty good too, considering it was brewed in a tin can and drunk from the same, passed back and forth across the dying fire. He asked her why she didn't carry more cultured cooking gear aboard her roomy-enough vessel. She shrugged and said, "Me sainted mother was from the Tinker Folk, which is why me father named his boat *The Irish Rover*. She raised me not to rely on vanities some tax collector will only steal from ye if the thieves don't first. She taught me to jist reach out for such pleasures of this cruel world as I had the chance to, in passing through it from cradle to grave."

She stared down at the dying embers for a moment before she looked up thoughtfully to ask, "So how long will we have for our pleasures before ye'll be laving Zion, Dick?"

He stared back at her soberly and replied, "We'll know in a little while if there'll even be a Zion to sail back to, Fionna. I think I may have sort of discouraged those guerrillas this afternoon. But if I failed, they'll be sending some noise our way from the river crossing. They'll attack between sunset and moonrise, if they mean to attack at all.''

"That wasn't the question I asked ye, Dick.''

"I know. You're a sweet kid, Fionna, and I'm a knockaround guy who never stays in one place long enough to matter. You see, there's a price on my head. I'm on the run. So I'm just bad news for decent women.''

"Och, I could see from the start ye was a traveling-on man. I didn't ask ye if ye'd be staying in Zion *forever,* Dick. I only asked how long we'd have together before ye moved on. And if ye're afraid of me begging to be after going on with ye, have no fear. For I've me own business to keep me here, I'm a wanderer's daughter, so I know the rules.''

He smiled gently at her and said, "Sometimes I wish they were different, too. Let's hold the thought while we wait for that damned sun to go down. If Zion's still there by morning, I suppose we'll be stuck there at least until the next coastal steamer south. Somehow I don't think my pal Gaston and me ought to go back to England with the others. But what about *you* and the evacuation, Kid? How can you stay on here if the colony's abandoned?''

She shrugged and replied, "Abandoned by who? I get along all right with the Dons; I like thim better than the auld English; and everyone eats fish. Getting back to more important matters, the next coastal schooner that stops here regularly will get here in about two weeks. Do ye think ye could stand me cooking that long, Dick?''

He grinned at her and said, "I guess I'll have to. But get back in the boat. I'll shove you off, and we can at least pole out to the far side. It'll be dark any minute, and if nobody can see us nobody can interrupt this interesting conversation no matter who just won the war.''

She picked up her frying pan, swished it in wet sand to sort of clean it and climbed into *The Irish Rover* with it. He admired the way she did the dishes. He got to his feet and put a bare shoulder to the bluff bow to shove the boat off. He followed it out, still shoving, till he had it moving good and the water was up around his waist. Then he pulled himself aboard too, to see how Fionna was following her sainted mother's instructions on living with just the bare essentials. Fionna was bare from head to toe as she reclined on the bedroll she'd hauled out to spread on the duckboards. He lay down beside her to take her in his arms as the boat went on gliding across the lagoon in the sunset. By the time it came to a gentle halt two-thirds of the way across the lagoon, he was in her—and her movements under him weren't gentle at all, but awfully nice.

Thanks to an earlier sexual adventure that afternoon which he was now thoroughly ashamed of, and thanks to how Fionna had begun this adventure hard up as hell, she came twice before he did and took his continued enthusiasm as a great compliment.

As the sun and his first passion subsided together, he lay still atop her in the gathering dusk, saying, "Let's be still a minute, Doll. It's not easy to listen to distant drumfire with your heels drumming on my behind like that."

She crooned, "Och, Dick, Dick, I don't care if we ever see another dawn again if ye'll promise me jist this night!"

"Hush, Honey. It's dark enough, now. I don't hear anything, and they'd have that cannon of theirs going by now if they hope to soften our guys up this side of moonrise, see?"

She did. She wasn't at all stupid, and now that she'd recovered from her first orgasms, she was interested enough in his other problems to listen with him. They lay there sweetly entwined in the bottom of *The Irish Rover*, moving just enough to stay friends, as all they heard was the gentle lapping of water against the hull and the chirping of crickets from the trees all around. He said, "Hot damn. I don't know how we did it. But if any of those bastards are still in the bandit business, it sounds as if they've taken their business somewhere else!"

She moved languorously under him as she said, "I'm glad. But I'm not too surprised, for if that wasn't thunder I heard before, ye sure made enough noise to drive most bandits out of business, Dear. Did ye foind out anything about them hostages ye were worried about while ye was tearing their pub apart?''

He grimaced and said, ''Enough to tell the governor not to worry about them anymore. There's no sense trying to separate the sheep from the goats now that they're gone. May as well let their kith and kin think *all* of them were good guys.''

He started moving in her again. Fionna sweetly wrapped her strong young limbs around him to lend him a helping pelvis. But the trouble with starting a conversation with a woman at times like these was that, once you got a woman talking and screwing at the same time, they could carry on at both ends and seemed to like to. Fionna moaned, ''Och, I like it when ye'd be after hitting bottom like that, Darling. But tell me something. Ye said your friends had no great guns, and ye said it was only a machine gun ye were after firing at the dorty sods in town. So what made all them great bangs I heard while I was waiting for ye here?''

He wanted to bang her more than he wanted to explain military tactics. So he kissed her, laughed and said, ''Oh, let's just say you heard the bombs of Gilead.''